THIS Book Belongs

To

THE SILVER PRINCESS IN OZ

The SILVER PRINCESS *in* OZ

By
RUTH PLUMLY THOMPSON
Founded on and continuing the Famous Oz Stories

By
L. FRANK BAUM
"Royal Historian of Oz"

Illustrated by
JOHN R. NEILL

NEW YORK
Books of Wonder
1996

THE SILVER PRINCESS IN OZ
Copyright 1938
By
THE REILLY & LEE CO.
Printed in the U. S. A.

This new edition published by
Books of Wonder
16 West 18th Street
New York, NY 10011

Printed in the U.S.A.

ISBN 0-929605-56-X

1 2 3 4 5 6 7 8 9

Dear Boys and Girls:

This book will tell you all that happened when Randy and Kabumpo traveled off to the Castle of the Red Jinn. Halfway there they met a Princess from Anuther Planet and her Thunder Colt; later, a villain named Gludwig. With a name like that, we'd know he was a villain, wouldn't we? Now DO tell me what interested you most in this story; any Oz news you have heard lately and all about yourself!

There goes the bell now! Well, I'm expecting a merry message any minute from any of you! Exciting, isn't it? So here I go to read my first letter!

Yours, with last year's love and this year's wishes!

RUTH PLUMLY THOMPSON

254 S. Farragut Terrace,
West Philadelphia, Pa.

PUBLISHER'S NOTE

This book was first published in 1938 and reflects some ideas and biases which were deemed acceptable at that time, but have since been repudiated by a more enlightened genereation. The original text and illustrations are presented here in their entirety for the purpose of historical accuracy and to maintain the book's authenticity. The views expressed herein, however, in no way reflect those of the publisher, nor are condoned by them.

To two Little Girls
FLORENCE LINN EDSALL
and
MARY JOSEPHINE RITCHIE
this book is lovingly dedicated
by their cousin
RUTH.

LIST OF CHAPTERS

CHAPTER		PAGE
1	The King Rebels	17
2	The Elegant Elephant of Oz	28
3	Gaper's Gulch	41
4	Out of Gaper's Gulch	54
5	Headway	64
6	The Other Side of the Desert	80
7	The Princess of Anuther Planet	94
8	On to Ev	112
9	The Box Wood	128
10	Night in the Forest	143
11	The Field of Feathers	157
12	Arrival at the Castle of the Red Jinn	169
13	Gludwig the Glubrious	184
14	The Slave of the Magic Dinner Bell	193
15	Nonagon Island	207
16	All Together at Last	217
17	In the Red Jinn's Castle	226
18	The Red Jinn Restored	236
19	Red Magic	241
20	King and Queen of Regalia	253

CHAPTER 1

The King Rebels

IN a far-away northwestern corner of the Gilliken
Country of Oz lies the rugged little Kingdom of
Regalia, and in an airy and elegant castle, set high
on the tallest mountain, lives Randy, its brave young
King. When the Regalians are not busy celebrating
one of their seventy-seven national holidays, they
are busy tending their flocks of goats or looking after
the vines that cover every mountain and hill, produc-
ing the largest and most luscious grapes in Oz. These
proud and independent mountain folk have much to
recommend them, and if they consider themselves

17

superior to any and all of the other natives in Oz, we must not blame them too much. Perhaps the sharp, clear air and high altitude in which they live is responsible for their top-lofty attitude. Randy, it must be confessed, found the stiff and unbending manner of his subjects and their correct and formal behavior on all occasions stuffy in the extreme; and of all the stuffy occasions he had to endure the week-ly court reception was the stuffiest. Just as I started this story he was winding up another of these royal and boring affairs.

"Hail! Hail! Give Majesty its proper due,
Hail Randywell, King Handywell of Brandenburg
and Bompadoo!
Boom! BOOM! BOOM!"

At each crash of the drums the young King winced and shuddered, then, pulling himself together, he nodded resignedly to his richly attired courtiers and subjects who were retiring backwards from the royal presence. As the last bowing figure swished through the double doors, Randy gave a huge sigh and groan. This was his three hundred and tenth reception since ascending the throne. Ahead stretched hundreds more, besides the daily courts where he acted as pre-siding Judge to settle all disputes of the realm;

18

countless reviewings of troops; inspections of model goat farms; and attendance at numerous celebrations for national heroes of Regalia.

"Oh, being a King is awful," choked the youthful monarch, loosening his regal cape and letting it fall unheeded to the floor. "AWFUL! Will it always be like this, Uncle?"

"Like what?" His uncle, the Grand Duke Hoochafoo, who was still inclining his head mechanically in the direction of the door, caught himself abruptly in the middle of a bow.

"Oh, all this silly standing round and being bowed at, this 'Hail! Hail! and Way for His Majesty!' stuff. Galloping Gollopers, Uncle, I'd like to step out by myself occasionally without twenty footmen springing to open doors and fifty pages tooting on their blasted trumpets. Why, I cannot even cross the courtyard, that a dozen guardsmen do not fall in behind me!" Flouncing over to the window, Randy stared out over the royal terrace. "Even the goats on the mountain have more fun than I do," he observed bitterly. "They can run, jump, climb and even butt one another, while I—" Randy let his arms fall heavily at his sides. "I have not even anyone to fight with. If just ONCE somebody would punch me in

19

the nose instead of bowing." Randy clenched and unclenched his fists.

"Hm—mm! So that's what you want!" Looking quizzically at his young nephew, Uncle Hoochafoo crossed to the bell rope and gave it a savage tug. As Randy's personal servant and valet appeared to an-

swer the ring, he spoke sharply, "Dawkins, kindly hit His Majesty in the nose!"

"The nose? Oh, but Your Lordship, I couldn't do a thing like that. 'Tisn't right, nor fitting—nor—"

"I said hit him in the nose," commanded Uncle Hoochafoo, advancing grimly upon the terrified valet.

"Yes, yes, like this!" Bringing up his fist, Randy

made such a splendid connection with the valet's nose, Dawkins toppled over backwards. Dancing from one foot to the other as the outraged servant sprang to his feet, Randy prepared to defend himself. But with his hand clapped to his nose, Dawkins was retiring rapidly. "Thank you!" he muttered in a strangled voice, "thank you very much!"

"Did you hear that? He said 'Thank you,' " screamed Randy as Dawkins disappeared with an agitated bow. "Oh, this is too much; I wish I were back with Nandywog in Tripedalia—or anywhere but here, doing anything but this."

"Now, now! Don't take things so hard," begged his uncle, patting him kindly on the shoulder.

"Hard?" Randy glared at the old nobleman. "I can take things hard, Uncle, but I cannot take them soft. I'll never forgive my father for getting me into this—NEVER!" Randy's father, former King of Regalia, tiring of a royal life and routine, had retired to a distant cave to live the life of a hermit, and Randy, after traveling all over Oz to fulfil the seven difficult tests required of a Regalian ruler, had succeeded to the throne.

"You should not speak like that of your royal parent," chided Uncle Hoochafoo, tapping his spectacles absently against his teeth, "for you are very much like him, my boy, very much like him. Hmm! Hmm! Harumph!" Uncle Hoochafoo cleared his throat thoughtfully. "What you need is a change, a new interest. Ah, I have it! You must marry, my lad, you must marry! Some pretty little Princess or rich

young Queen, and then everything will be punjanoobious!"

"Is being married anything like being a King?" inquired Randy suspiciously.

"Oh, no. No, indeed, quite the reverse." The eyes of the old Duke, who had once been married, grew glazed and pensive. "Once you are married, you will feel less like a King every day," he promised solemnly. "And the arguments alone will keep you occupied for hours." Uncle Hoochafoo raised both shoulders and eyebrows. "Wait, I'll just go consult the wise men about a proper Princess for you."

"No! No! I do not wish to be married," announced Randy, stamping his foot. "I'll not marry for years," he declared stubbornly. Then, as loud outcries and tremendous thumps interrupted them, he hurried over to an open window just in time to meet a large rock that came crashing through the amethyst pane.

"Look out!" blustered Uncle Hoochafoo, jerking Randy to his feet, for the rock had completely bowled him over. "Well, I see you have your wish. How's that for a knock in the nose, my lad? Not only the nose, but also the beginning of a beautiful black eye!"

"Have I really?" Racing over to a mirror, Randy proudly examined his injured orb. "Oh, Uncle, isn't this fun? Who did it? What's up, d'ye s'pose—a revolution?" Hurrying back to the window, Randy recklessly thrust out his head to stare down into the courtyard. Kayub, the Gatekeeper, had his shoulder braced against the gold-studded doors in the castle wall, but even so, the doors were bulging and creaking from the thunderous blows struck from the other side.

"Open in the name of the LAW!" boomed a tremendous voice. "Thump! Thump! Kerbang! OPEN in the name of a Prince of the Realm! Open this door, you unmannerly Scuppernong!"

"No, no, stay where you are!" panted Kayub, waving desperately with one arm for the guards to come help him. "Stay where you are, or go to the rear

entrance! Who do you think you are, hammering on the doors of His Majesty's castle?"

"I don't think, I know!" raged the voice from the other side of the wall. "I am a Prince of Pumperdink, you unspeakable clod. Open up this door before I break it down!" And after even more furious thumps another shower of rocks came flying over the wall.

"Great Gillikens! I think—I believe—why it IS! Kayub, Kayub, open the door! It is a Prince!" shouted Randy, using both hands as a megaphone.

" 'Tis nothing of the sort," grunted the Gatekeeper obstinately. "I looked through me little grill but a moment ago and it's no Prince at all, but a parade! A parade of one elephant, if you please, and when I orders him to the rear entrance he ups with his trunk and flings rocks over our wall!"

"But this elephant IS a Prince," insisted Randy, banging on the window ledge. "Besides, he's a great friend of mine."

"Open the door, fool!" directed Uncle Hoochafoo, leaning so far out the window his crown fell to the paving stones. "The King has spoken. Admit this elephant at once! At once!"

"And about time," fumed an indignant voice, as Kayub reluctantly drew the bolts and, swinging wide the doors, stepped back to let a magnificently caparisoned elephant swing through. "A fine welcome this is, I must say, for the Elegant Elephant of Oz! Out of my way, wart!" Picking Kayub up in his trunk, the visitor jammed him down hard into a golden trash barrel, trumpeted fiercely at the double line of guards who had instantly sprung to attention, and went swaying across the courtyard.

Now nowhere but in Oz could an elephant talk, much less come hammering on the doors of a royal castle, but in Oz, as we very well know, animals talk and act as sensibly as people, which makes Oz about ten times as exciting as any other country on the map. But while I've been explaining all this,

Randy had run down the steps and was half-way across the courtyard.

"Kabumpo, KABUMPO, is it really you? Oh, at last—AT LAST you are here!" Impatiently waving aside the guards, Randy led his mammoth and still muttering guest into the palace.

"Kaybumpo, is it?" sniffed Kayub, jerking him-

self with great difficulty out of the trash barrel.
"Such goings on. Well, all I say—" The Gatekeeper
peered carefully over his shoulder to see that the
elephant was safely inside the castle, then, raising
his arm for the benefit of the staring guards, he
cried fiercely. "All I can say is—just let him show
his snoot around here again and I'll kabump him
down the mountain!"

CHAPTER 2

The Elegant Elephant of Oz

FORTUNATELY the doors of Randy's castle were high and wide, and the rooms so large and spacious, even a guest as large as this elephant could quite easily be accommodated. Still irritated by the Gatekeeper's insolence, Kabumpo followed the young ruler to the throne room where he sank stiffly to his haunches and waited in outraged silence for Randy to speak. Randy, however, was so surprised and happy to see his old friend and comrade, he could not utter a word. But the Elegant Elephant could not long withstand the honest delight **and**

28

affection beaming from the young King's eyes, and under that kindly glow his wrath melted away like fog in the sunshine.

"Well! Well!" he rumbled testily, "how do I look?"

"Elegant!" breathed Randy, stepping back to have a better view. "Elegant as ever. You've worn your best robe and jewels, haven't you?"

"Always wear my best when I call on a King," said Kabumpo, smoothing down his embroidered collar complacently with his trunk.

"And I believe you've grown a foot," went on Randy, standing on tiptoe to pat Kabumpo on the shoulder.

"A foot," roared the Elegant Elephant, throwing back his head. "Oh, come now, I couldn't have grown a foot without noticing it, and I still have but four—here, count 'em! Say, who in hay bales gave you that black eye?"

"YOU did." Randy fairly sputtered with mirth at Kabumpo's discomfited expression. "I was just wishing someone would hit me in the nose, when along came that rock and NOW look at me!"

"Yes," put in Uncle Hoochafoo, regarding Kabumpo severely through his monocle. "Now look at him!"

"Well, why didn't you tell that wart of a door-keeper I was expected?" demanded Kabumpo explosively.

"The King of Regalia does not hold conversation with his doorkeeper," explained Randy's uncle, giving the Elegant Elephant a very sour look.

"Oh, he doesn't!" Kabumpo lurched grandly to

his feet. "Well, it's time somebody told him about the Elegant Elephant of Oz and how he should be received and welcomed. Let me tell you, sirrah—trumpets blow when I come and go in Pumperdink!"

"Then why did you ever leave there?" inquired the Duke coldly.

"Oh, Uncle, don't you remember, we were to review the Purple Guard at five? YOU go," urged

Randy, fearful lest the tempery old Duke would still further insult the even more tempery old elephant. "Honestly, I feel a cold coming on." Randy coughed plaintively, at the same time winking at Kabumpo.

"Very well, I'll go," agreed his uncle stiffly. "But do not forget there is a dinner for the Grape Growers at seven, a concert of the Goat Herdsmen at eight, maneuvers of our Highland Guards in the Royal Barracks at nine and—"

"Yes, yes! All right!" Randy fairly pushed his royal relative toward the door.

"An ancient pest if I ever saw one," grumbled Kabumpo as the Grand Duke disappeared with a very grim expression. "Great gooselberries! Do we have to do all those dumb things? Why, it's six years since I've seen you, Randy, and I kinda thought we'd have a cozy time all to ourselves."

"I never have any time to myself," sighed the young monarch wistfully. "I do nothing but lay cornerstones and raise flags and stand around at Royal Courts and Receptions. Everybody bows and bows. Why, it's got so I even bow to myself when I look in the glass, and NOW—" Randy raised his arms indignantly. "Now Uncle Hoochafoo says I must marry."

31

"Marry!" trumpeted Kabumpo, twinkling his eyes angrily. "What nonsense! Why, you are nowhere near old enough to marry. You were only about ten when I met you and that makes you sixteen now, though I must say you don't look it!"

"Oh, no one in Oz looks his age," grinned Randy, "and you know I'd been ten for about four years before I knew you, Kabumpo, so that makes me twenty or so, doesn't it?"

"I don't care what it makes you," rumbled Kabumpo, "it makes me mad. And to think I actually helped get you into all this boring business. My ears and trunk, Kingling, it's up to me to get you out of it."

"How?" demanded Randy, folding his arms and leaning despondently against the mantel. "How does one stop being a King, Kabumpo?"

"Why, by stopping," announced the Elegant Elephant, spreading his ears to their fullest extent. "By taking a vacation, my fine young sprig. By departing and going hence for a suitable season. Do you suppose I came all the way from Pumperdink to hear Goatherds tootling on bells and Highlanders tramping round a barracks? I came to see you, my boy, and nobody else." Kabumpo paused to blow his

32

trunk explosively on a violet silk handkerchief. "And after that I thought we'd go and visit the Red Jinn."

"Oh, Kabumpo, could we?" Randy's face brightened and then as quickly fell. "I don't believe Uncle Hoochafoo will let me go," he finished dolefully.

"A King does not ask whether or not he may go, he GOES," stated the Elegant Elephant, beginning to sway like a ship under full sail. "But to avoid all arguments we'll not start till later. Could you be ready by midnight, young one?"

"Oh, I'm ready now," declared Randy, picking up his cloak from the floor and snatching a sword from its bracket on the wall. "Why ever did you wait so long, Kabumpo? You promised to visit me six months after I was crowned."

"Well, you know how it is at a court." The Elegant Elephant sighed and settled back on his haunches again. "If it isn't one thing it's another, but here I am at last. So—order up your dinner and a few bales of hay and a barrel of cider for me. I crave rest and refreshment."

"And what about the Grape Growers, the Goatherds and Highlanders?" worried Randy.

"Oh, them!" exclaimed Kabumpo inelegantly.

33

"Here!" Seizing a pen from the royal desk, he scribbled a defiant message on a handy piece of parchment.

"No admittance under extreme penalty of the Law. Do not disturb! By special order of His Maj-

esty, King Randywell Handywell of Brandenburg and Bompadoo."

"See, I remembered all your names, and I've used them all!" Opening the door with his trunk, Kabumpo impaled the notice on the knob, then quietly closed the door and turned the key in the lock. And only once did they open it, and then to admit ten flustered footmen with Randy's dinner and Kabumpo's cider and hay. To imperious raps, taps and numerous notes thrust under the door by the young

King's agitated uncle, they paid no attention whatever. They were too busy talking over old times and the exciting days when they had journeyed all over Oz, and with the help of Jinnicky, the little Red Jinn, saved the Royal Family of Pumperdink from the Witch of Follensby Forest.

Pumperdink, as most of you know, is in the north central part of the Gilliken Country of Oz, and ruled by King Pompus and Queen Posy. Their son, Prince Pompadore, has much to say about affairs in that Kingdom, but it is to Kabumpo, his Elegant Elephant, that Pompus turned oftenest for counsel and comfort. Given to the King by a celebrated Blue Emperor, Kabumpo has proved himself so wise and sagacious, Pompus depends on him for almost everything. It is Kabumpo who advises His Majesty when to have his hair cut and put aside his woolen underwear, when to go to the dentist, when to turn in his old four-horse chariot for a twelve-horse model, when to save money—when to spend it, how to get on with neighboring Kings and how to get on without them. In fact, so heavy are the duties and responsibilities of this remarkable elephant, 'tis a wonder, even after six years, he managed this visit to Randy.

Randy's first meeting with Kabumpo had been more or less by chance. Sent out disguised as a poor mountain boy to pass the seven severe tests of King-ship required of Regalian Rulers, Randy had hap-pened to come first to the Kingdom of Pumperdink and had been hailed before the King as a vagrant.

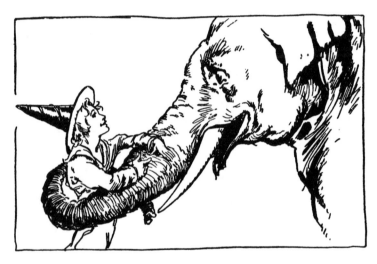

The Elegant Elephant, taking an instant fancy to the boy, had insisted that he be allowed to stay on as his own royal attendant, and in this comical ca-pacity Randy's adventures had begun. For scarcely had he been in the palace of Pumperdink a week, before Kettywig, the King's brother, and the Witch of Follensby Forest, plotting to steal the crown, caused the whole royal family to disappear by some strange and fiery magic. Barely missing the same fate, Randy and Kabumpo managed to escape. On their way through the forest they met a Soothsayer who told them to seek out the Red Jinn. Now no one in Oz had ever heard of this singular personage, but after many delays and hair-raising experiences,

Randy and Kabumpo finally arrived at his splendid red glass castle. Jinnicky, it turned out, was the Wizard of Ev, and a merry and strange person he was. Jinnicky's whole body is encased in a shiny red jar into which he can retire like a turtle at will, and the little Wizard's disposition is so gay and jolly everyone around him feels the same way. Not only did he welcome his visitors, but set off immediately to help the Royal Family of Pumperdink out of their misfortunes and enchantment. Once in Pumperdink, Randy, with the help of the Red Jinn's magic looking-glasses, was able to trace the lost King and his family and release them from the witch's spell. But before that, and while he was traveling here and there with Kabumpo and Jinnicky, the little Prince was fulfilling all the tests and conditions required by the ancient laws of Regalia of their Kings. In other words, he had made three true friends, served a strange King, saved a Queen, showed bravery in battle, overcome a fabulous monster, disenchanted a Princess, and received from a Wizard an important magic treasure. And now, looking back on those brave, bright days, he could not help thinking that earning his crown had been more fun than wearing it.

"I wish we could do it all over again," he mused, as Kabumpo, after recalling their visit to Nandywog, the little giant, tossed off the last of the cider.

"But think where we're going now," gurgled Kabumpo, setting down the barrel with a resounding thud. "If something strange or exciting does not happen on the way there or back, or in Jinnicky's castle itself, I do not know my Oz and Evistery.

Can't you just see Jinnicky's face when we arrive? I wonder if Alibabble is still Grand Advizier and if the magic dinner bell is still working. Yes! Yes? Who's there?" Kabumpo raised his voice irritably as a persistent whistling came through the keyhole.

"It's Dawkins," explained an anxious voice from the other side of the door. "The Duke says as it's high time His Highness was in bed, Your Highness!"

"Oh, be off with you. Go dive in the feathers yourself. His Highness is going to sleep in here on the floor." Kabumpo stood so close and spoke so violently through the keyhole, Dawkins was blown back against the opposite wall. For a time footsteps pattered up and down the corridor, then finally deciding the young King was to have his own way at last,

the footmen and courtiers and even Uncle Hoochafoo
took themselves off. But not till everything was absolutely quiet and still and everyone in the castle
asleep did Kabumpo and Randy venture forth. Then,
stepping softly as his own tremendous shadow, the
Elegant Elephant with the young King on his back
slipped through the silent halls and deserted courtyard, past the snoring sentries and keeper of the
gate and on out into the foresty Highlands beyond
the palace wall. Here in the bright white light of a
smiling moon they took the highway to the north,
for the castle of the Red Jinn lies to the north by
northeast of Regalia and Oz.

"How'll we cross the Deadly Desert?" murmured
Randy, drowsily clutching the few belongings he had
tied up in an old silver table-cloth. In it he had his
oldest suit, some clean underwear, his tooth brush
and his trusty sword.

"Never cross a desert till you come to it," advised
Kabumpo. "And we've crossed it before, you know."

"Yes, I know." Smiling to himself, Randy dropped
his head on his bundle, and lulled by the agreeable
motion of his gigantic bearer, soon fell asleep, to
dream pleasantly of Alibabble and of Ginger, slave
of the Red Jinn's dinner bell.

CHAPTER 3

Gaper's Gulch

KABUMPO, as happy to escape from Court life as Randy, moved rhythmically as a ship through the soft spring night. Humming to himself and busy with his own thoughts, he scarcely noticed that the highway was growing steeper and narrower until he was brought up sharp by an impassable barrier of rock.

"Now, Bosh and Botherskites! I was sure this road ran straight to the Deadly Desert," he muttered, reaching back with his trunk to see that Randy was still safely aboard and asleep. "Beets and butter-

41

nuts! Do I have to turn back, or plough through all this rubble?" The Elegant Elephant's small eyes twinkled with irritation, and easing himself to the right off the highway, he peered crossly up at the offending mass of stone. Finding no way round here, he swung over to the left and examined it closely from that side, and was just about to start resignedly through the brush when he discovered that what he had taken for an especially dark shadow was really a cleft in the rock. It was barely wide enough for him to squeeze through without scraping the jewels from his robe. "Now then, shall I risk it or wait till morning?" mused Kabumpo, swaying undecidedly to and fro. "It might take us straight through to the other side of the highway. On the other trunk, it might lead into a robber's cave or plunge us suddenly over a precipice!"

Edging closer, the Elegant Elephant thrust his trunk into the crevice. It seemed smooth and solid, and, resolved to try it even though little of the moonlight penetrated into the narrow opening, Kabumpo stepped inside and proceeded to pick his way cautiously along the rocky corridor. For about the length of a city street it ran straight ahead, then curved sharply to the right. Here Kabumpo was heartened to see a lantern hanging from an iron spike, while carved on the smooth rock below was a blunt message.

"This is the entrance to Gaper's Gulch. Pause here and give three yawns and a stretch for Sleeperoo, Great, Grand and Most Snorious Gaper!"

"Snorious Gaper! Ho, Ho! kerumph! Who ever heard of such nonsense?" snorted Kabumpo, squinting impatiently down at the notice. "Ah, Hah! HOH, HUM!" At this point, and without seeming able to help it, the Elegant Elephant yawned so terrifically his head-piece fell over one ear, and his jaw was almost dislocated. To recover his dignity and with tears starting from his eyes, he gave himself a quick shake, then stretched up his trunk to straighten his headgear.

"Splen—did!" drawled a sleepy voice. "You may now proceed as before." Blinking angrily about to see who had addressed him, the Elegant Elephant spied a round-faced and widely gaping guard standing in a little niche in the rock. Strapped to his shoulders, instead of a knapsack, was a fat feather pillow, and as Kabumpo came opposite the guard's eyes closed, and falling back against his cushion he began gently to snore. As Kabumpo stopped in some astonishment,

43

the guard's nap was rudely interrupted by a pailful of pebbles that cascaded merrily down over his ears. There were twenty pails operating on a moving belt above his head and at three-minute intervals they pelted him awake, as Kabumpo presently discovered. The buttons on the guard's uniform were illuminated and spelled out his name, "WINKS."

"Well, do I surprise you?" inquired Winks, shak-

ing the pebbles from his shoulders and rubbing his eyes with his yellow-gloved hands. Kabumpo, too amused to speak, nodded.

"And you surprise me," admitted the guard, gaping three times just to prove it, "you big, enormous, impossible whatever you are—you! Why, you should have been underground months ago! But that'll all be taken care of," he added smoothly. "Just follow the arrows and you cannot miss—just follow the arrows—just fol—"

As Kabumpo, fuming from what he considered a mortal insult, lunged forward, the little soldier's eyes fell shut again. Held more by curiosity than by a desire to continue the conversation, Kabumpo waited for the next bucket of pebbles to shower over the guard.

" 'Low the arrows," went on Winks as calmly as if he had not been interrupted at all. "There are forty guards to point the way. Forty Winks," he repeated, closing one eye. "Ha, Ha! To point the way. Ha, Ha! HOH, HUM! Do you get the point?"

As Kabumpo started off with a little snort of disgust, he felt a slight prick in his left hind leg, for Winks, just as he feel asleep, let fly an arrow from his old-fashioned bow. Before Kabumpo had reached the end of the passageway he had passed forty of the Gaper Guards. After his experience with the first, he did not stop for further talk, but made the best speed possible, resolved to rush through Gaper's Gulch when he came to it without even pausing to

45

express his contempt. The pebble awakeners were so neatly timed, each guard had a chance to speed an arrow after the flying elephant, and by the time Kabumpo reached the opening at the other end of the rocky pass, he had forty arrows pricking through his robe or stuck here and there in his ears and ankles. With his tough hide, they hurt no more than pin pricks, but vastly indignant at such treatment, the Elegant Elephant began jerking them out with his trunk.

"What do they think I am, a pincushion? Hoh!" he snorted, pulling out the last one, and relieved to note that Randy had escaped the missiles entirely. Indeed, the young King of Regalia was sleeping as placidly as if he were home in his own castle. Kabumpo, too, felt unaccountably drowsy, and as he pushed his way down into the rocky little glen his steps grew slower and slower. So far as he could see by the light of the fast waning moon, there were neither houses nor people in Gaper's Gulch. In the center of the valley the rough stones and brush had been cleared away and a series of flat rocks were spaced out almost like a gigantic checker-board. Pausing beside the largest rock, Kabumpo spelled out the name of Sleeperoo the Great and Snorious.

"What is this, a cemetery?" gulped the Elegant Elephant. "But that could not be, for no one in Oz ever dies. Ho, Hum!"

Leaning up against a dead pine and blinking furiously to keep awake, he pondered the unpleasant situation. Then, deciding that, cemetery or not, he must have some sleep, he lifted Randy down from

his back and rolled him in a blanket he had thoughtfully brought along. Then, divesting himself of his jeweled robe and head-piece, Kabumpo stretched out carefully beside his young comrade and in twenty minutes was fast asleep.

How long he slumbered Kabumpo never knew, but from a nightmare in which he was struggling in a bank of treacherous quicksand, he awoke with a frightful sinking feeling to find he was surrounded by forty more of the Gaper Guards. Their buttons

were also lit up and on each plump chest he could read the word "Wake." The Wakes were busily at work with pick and spade, and, unlike the Winks, did not seem the least bit drowsy. Half convinced he was still asleep and dreaming, Kabumpo peered out at them through half-closed lids, then gave a tremendous grunt. Great Gillikens! He was sinking! The busy little Wakes had dug a trench at least twenty feet deep all around him and now, careless of their own safety, were shoveling away at the mound on which he was still precariously resting.

"Quick, a few more to the right," directed a crisp little voice. "Watch yourself there, Torpy. Ah, here he comes! Heads up, lads!"

As the Chief Wake spoke, Kabumpo felt the mound give way and down he rolled into the pit, while the Wakes scrambled frantically up the sides.

"Did you hear that fierce TOOT?" puffed the little Guard addressed as Torpy. "It's awake, fellows! What's wrong with those sleeping arrows—don't they work any more? I myself saw forty sticking in the big Whatisit when he came pounding out of the pass. Hurry, hurry! let's get him under ground!" And, seizing their picks and spades again, the Gaper Guards began shoveling dirt into the pit, paying no attention to Kabumpo's furious blasts and bellows, which grew wilder and more anguished as he suddenly realized that Randy was no longer beside him.

"What have you done with the boy? Halt! Stop! How dare you cast dirt on an Imperial Prince of Pumperdink or try to bury the Elegant Elephant of Oz?"

Shaking the mud from his head and raising his

trunk, Kabumpo let out such an ear-splitting trumpet, twenty Wakes fell to their knees, and the others dropped pick and shovel and stared at him in positive dismay.

"But, sir, it is quite customary to bury all visitors," quavered Torpy as soon as he could make himself heard. "We'll dig you up in six months and you'll be good as new. Our dormitories are so very comfortable, and all Gapers lie dormant for six months!"

"But I'm not a GAPER," screamed Kabumpo, interrupting himself with a yawn both wide and gusty.

"Oh, but you soon will be," asserted Torpy, squinting down at him earnestly. "Why, you're gaping already. Now lie down like a good beast. Sleeping underground is lovely."

"LOVELY!" repeated all the rest of the Wakes, beginning to croon as they shoveled. Kabumpo, opening his mouth to protest again, caught a bushel of earth between his tusks and, half choked and blind with rage, the Elegant Elephant hurled himself at the side of the pit. He could almost reach the top with his trunk and, as the Wakes squealing with alarm shoveled faster and faster, he wound his trunk round an old tree stump and by main strength hauled himself up over the edge.

"NOW!" he bellowed, spreading his ears like sails. "Where have you buried the boy? Quick, speak up or I'll pound you to splinters."

Snatching a log in his trunk, Kabumpo surged forward. But the terrified Wakes, instead of answering, fled for their lives, leaving Kabumpo all alone in the ghostly little valley.

"Randy! Randy, where are you? Oh, my poor boy, are you suffocated?"

Galloping this way and that, Kabumpo peered desperately about for a patch of newly turned earth. But only the wind whistling drearily through the dead branches of the pine trees came to answer him. Frantic with worry, the Elegant Elephant began pounding with his log on the headstones of the dormant Gapers, trumpeting at the same time in a way to wake the dead.

CHAPTER 4

Out of Gaper's Gulch

NOW the Gapers were not dead, but only sleeping, and soon the dormant natives of this strange Hiber-nation lifted up their headstones and began blinking out indignantly to see what and who had got loose in their quiet valley.

"Silence! Cease! Desist!" shuddered Sleeperoo the Great and Snorious, holding up his headstone with one hand and waving his other arm feebly at Kabumpo. "A bit more of that racket and we'll be roused for months. Who are you? And what is the meaning of all this Hah Hoh Humbuggery?"

Gaping ten times in quick succession, Sleeperoo

stuck out his lip at the Elegant Elephant. Kabumpo, startled by the spectacle of a hundred lifted headstones and the round dirty moonlike faces gaping up at him, said nothing for a whole minute. Then, stepping over to the Chief Gaper, he burst out angrily:

"I am a traveler whom your guards stuck full of arrows and then tried to bury. The young King who was with me has disappeared. I, the Elegant Elephant of Oz and Pumperdink, DEMAND his release. What have you done with the King of Regalia? Produce him at once, or I'll stand here and trumpet till doomsday!"

To show he meant what he said, Kabumpo let out such a terrific blast the headstones of his listeners rocked and shivered.

"Oh, my head! My ears! My ears, my dears! Give him what he's yelling for," sobbed Sleeperoo, crouching under his headstone as Kabumpo lifted his trunk for another trumpet.

"Is this—a—king?" called a fretful voice, and, lurching round, Kabumpo saw a fat old Gaper now halfway above ground. Balancing his stone on his fat head, he held Randy out at arm's length. "Instead of digging him a proper bed, they stuck him in

55

with me," he complained. "Here, take him—he kicks like a mule and I can't abide a kicker." With a relieved grunt, Kabumpo snatched Randy from the Gaper's damp clutches, thankful the boy still had strength enough to kick. Randy's face was quite pale and covered with dirt, but after a few anxious shakes he opened his eyes and looked confusedly round him.

"It's nothing," sniffed Kabumpo. "It's quite all right, my boy. You've just been buried to the ears and sleeping with a ground-hog."

"Buried?" shivered Randy, as Kabumpo set him gently on his back.

"Not buried at all, just lying dormant as a sensible body should," corrected the old Gaper, dropping out of sight with a slam of his headstone.

"Go away! Please go away!" begged Sleeperoo, as Kabumpo began stepping gingerly between the stones. "You're ruining our rest, you big bullying Behemoth!"

"I'll not stir a step till you send a guide to lead me out of this gulch," declared Kabumpo. "Call a guard or I'll call one myself."

"No. No! Please NOT! Torpy Snorpy—I say, Torpy," wheezed Sleeperoo, stretching up his thin neck. "Come, come all of you at once. At ONCE!"

As quickly as they had vanished, the Wakes slid from behind boulders and trees and up out of rocky crevices, their buttons twinkling cheerfully in the dark.

"Conduct these travelers to the head of the valley," ordered Sleeperoo, with a weak wave at the Gaper Guards.

"I thought this was a gulch," yawned Kabumpo,

while Randy began to shake the dirt from his hair and ears.

"A gulch is a valley," sniffed Sleeperoo, lowering himself crossly. "Look it up in any pictionary. A gulch is a valley or chasm."

"And Gaper's Gulch is a yawning chasm," mumbled Kabumpo, as the Chief Gaper and all the others began ducking back into their holes like rabbits into warrens. "Good night to you," he added, as the last stone slammed down. "Now, then, you boys fetch my head-piece and robe from that pit and let's start on."

Kabumpo spoke so sharply ten Wakes sprang to obey, and after they had brought them and both had been adjusted to Kabumpo's liking, he signaled

imperiously for Torpy and Snorpy to lead the way, and their companions took thankfully to their heels. For a while the two little Wakes marched ahead in a subdued silence as the Elegant Elephant picked his way around rocks and tree stumps.

"Not mad, I hope?" Torpy, most talkative of the two, looked anxiously over his shoulder.

"No, no—certainly not. I don't know when I've spent a more delightful evening," Kabumpo said. "Being stuck full of arrows and then buried alive is such splendid entertainment."

"Oh, I say now, we cannot all be alike," put in Snorpy, coming to the rescue of his embarrassed companion. "If those arrows had taken effect, you'd have been dead asleep before we buried you, and known nothing for six months. That's a lot of sleep to miss, Mister—er—Mister?"

"Kabumpo," chuckled Randy, who was now wide awake and quite recovered from his harrowing experience. "But you see, Kabumpo and I sleep every night and not all in one stretch as you do."

"More trouble that way," murmured Snorpy, shaking his head disapprovingly. "Keeps you hopping up and down all the time. In the Gulch we sleep half the year and then we are done with it."

"And what do you do when you are not sleeping?" inquired Kabumpo, stifling a yawn with his trunk.

"We eat," grinned Snorpy, his eyes twinkling brighter than his buttons. "Breakfast from July first to August thirty-first; lunch from September first till October thirty-first; and dinner from November first till New Year's."

59

"You mean you eat straight through without stopping?" gasped Randy, raising himself on one elbow. "All the time you're awake? Don't you ever work, play or go on journeys?"

"I do not know what you mean by 'work, play and going on journeys,' but whatever they are, we don't. We eat and sleep, sleep and eat and everything is perfectly gorgeous," confided the Wake with a satisfied skip.

"Gorging is gorgeous to some people, I suppose." Kabumpo tossed his head to show it was not his way. "Then how is it you fellows are not sleeping along with the other Gapers?"

"Oh, we're trained to sleep in summer and fall and to eat in winter and spring. The Winks are not so clever at staying awake as we are, but they'll learn, and meanwhile the pebbles keep them fairly active."

"Yes, active enough to shoot at visitors," grunted Kabumpo, winking back at Randy. "Do you shoot one another asleep or is that a special treat you reserve for travelers?"

"We just shoot at travelers," admitted Snorpy, quite cheerfully. "Otherwise they would interfere with our customs, interrupt our sleeping and eating and wake us up out of season."

"Just as we did," chuckled Randy. "I suppose we interrupted your dinner, this being one of the dinner months?" Both Guards nodded, exchanging pleased little smiles.

"Come on back and have a bite with us," invited Snorpy generously. "We've weak fish for the first week, chops for the second—"

Randy, tugging at Kabumpo's collar, begged him

to stop, for Randy was hungry as a brace of bears, but the Elegant Elephant, shaking his head till all his jewels rattled, declined the invitation with great firmness.

"No knowing what will come of it," he whispered to his disappointed young comrade. "Might put us to sleep for a century and it's about all I can do to keep my eyes open now. Wait till we're out of this goopy gulch, my lad, and we'll eat and sleep like gentlemen. After all, we are gentlemen and not ground-hogs."

Urging his guides to greater speed, the weary beast pushed doggedly on through the brush and stubble. Snorpy and Torpy, insulted by the shortness with which the Elegant Elephant had refused

their invitation, had little more to say, and in less than an hour had brought the travelers to the end of the rocky little valley. From where they stood, a crooked path wound crazily upward, and with a silent wave aloft the two Wakes turned and ran.

"Back to their dinner," sighed Randy, looking

hungrily after them. But Kabumpo, charmed to see the last of the ghostly gulch and its inhabitants, began to ascend the path, not even stopping for breath till he had come to the top. Even after this, he traveled on for about five miles to make sure no sleepy vapors or Gapers would trouble them again. The moon had waned and the stars grown faint as he stopped at last in a small patch of woodland. Here, without removing his head-piece or robe, Kabumpo braced his back against a mighty oak and fell asleep on his feet, and Randy, soothed and rocked by his tremendous snores, soon closed his eyes and slept also.

CHAPTER 5

Headway

WHEN Randy wakened, Kabumpo had already started on, grumbling under his breath, because nowhere in sight was there a green bush, a tree or anything at all that an elephant or little boy might eat.

"Where are we?" yawned Randy, sitting up and rubbing his eyes with his knuckles. "Great Gillikens, this is as bad as Gaper's Gulch!"

"All the countries bordering on the Deadly Desert are queer no-count little places," sniffed the Elegant Elephant, angrily jerking his robe off a cactus. "And

64

from the feel of the air, we must be near the desert now."

At mention of the Deadly Desert, Randy lapsed into an uneasy silence, for how could they ever cross this tract of burning sand, and how could they reach Ev or Jinnicky's castles unless they did cross it? While this vast belt of destroying sand effectively kept enemies out of Oz, it also kept the Ozians in.

"If we only had some of Jinnicky's magic or even his silver dinner bell to bring us a good breakfast!" sighed Randy, glancing round hungrily. "Pretty stupid of me not to have brought along a lunch, and there's not even a brook or stream in this miserable little patch of woods where a body could quench his thirst. Maybe it will rain, and that would help a little."

"Maybe," admitted Kabumpo, squinting up at the leaden sky. "Anyway, here we are out of the woods, but take a look at those rocks!"

"And those heads behind the rocks," whispered Randy, clutching Kabumpo's collar.

"There's something pretty odd about those heads, if you ask me," wheezed the Elegant Elephant, curling up his trunk. "Odd or I'm losing my eye and ear sight."

"Odd!" hissed Randy, tightening his hold on Kabumpo's collar. "Good goats and gravy! They're flying round loose like birds. Why, they've got no bodies on 'em, no bodies at all!"

"Read the sign," directed Kabumpo, uncurling his trunk and pointing to a crude warning scratched on a flat slab at the edge of the road leading to the rocky promontory above.

"Heads up! This road leads to Headland, nobody's allowed."

"Humph! Well, we won't make much headway without our bodies," grunted Kabumpo, as Randy read the message slowly to himself. "Such impudence! Why should we pay any attention to such stuff? Bodies or not, we're going on, and how can fellows minus feet and arms hope to stop us?"

"They might crash down on us with their heads," worried Randy, as an angry flock of Headmen circled round and round at the top of the road, "and those heads look hard."

"Not any harder than mine. Keep your crown on, Randy," advised Kabumpo grimly, "the spikes will dent 'em good, and if you reach down in my left-hand pocket you'll find a short club. The club will be better than your sword; you can't cut a head off

no neck and besides we don't really want to injure the pests. All ready? Then here we go!"

Randy did not answer, for hooking his heels through Kabumpo's harness, he was already delving into the capacious pocket on the left side of the Elegant Elephant's robe, discovering not only a club, but a quiver full of darts. Jerking himself upright, the club in one hand, the darts in the other, he peered aloft with growing anxiety as foot over foot Kabumpo climbed up the granite slope. The faces of the Headmen were round and deeply wrinkled from the hot winds blowing off the desert; their ears, huge and fan-shaped, flapped like wings, and like wings propelled them through the air. Before Kabumpo reached the top, a whole bevy came whizzing toward them, screaming out indignant threats and warnings.

"Off, be off!" they shouted hysterically. "Off with their arms, off with their legs, off with their bodies! Halt! Stop! Begone, you miserable creepy crawly creatures. You dare not set a foot on our beautiful Headland."

"Oh, daren't we?" Kabumpo shook his trunk belligerently. "And who is to stop us, pray?"

"I am," rasped the ugliest of the Headmen.

Snatching a coil of wire from a niche in the rocks with his teeth, the ugly little Mugly came flapping toward them. Another of the Headmen hastened to seize the opposite end of the wire in his teeth and, stretching it between them, they came rushing on.

"Watch out!" warned Randy, dropping flat between Kabumpo's ears. "They're going to trip you up."

"Wrong, how wrong," chattered all the Headmen, bobbing up and down like balloons let off their strings. "They're going to cut off his body," confided one of the long-nosed tribesmen, zooming down to whisper this information in Randy's ear. "The creature's head is welcome enough and with those enormous ears he'll have no trouble flying, but his body—oh, his body is awful and must stay behind. And your body, too, you little monster, we'll cut that off too," promised the Headman in his oily voice. "What use is a body, anyway? I see you have very small ears, but they can be stretched. And just wait till you've been debodicated, you'll feel so right and light and flighty."

"Help! Stop! Help! Help!" screamed Randy, as the ugly Mugly gave him a playful nip on the ear. "Back up, Kabumpo, back down. They're going to catch you in that wire and choke you."

69

"Pah! nonsense," panted the Elegant Elephant. And heaving himself up over the last barrier, he stepped confidently out on the rocky plateau.

"Heads up! Heads up!" shrilled the Headmen, while the two with the wire, deftly encircling Kabumpo's great neck, began to fly apart in order to draw the noose tighter. Kabumpo ducked, but much too late, and though his ferocious trumpeting sent swarms of Headmen fluttering aloft, the two holding the wire stuck to their task, pulling and jerking with all their teeth till Kabumpo's jeweled collar was pressing uncomfortably into his throat.

"Don't worry," he grunted gamely, "their teeth will give way before my neck does. Calm yourself, my boy, ca—alm your—self."

But how could Randy feel calm with his best friend in such a predicament and already beginning to gasp for breath? Jumping up and down on Kabumpo's back, he rattled his club valiantly, but the Headmen were too high up for him to reach, and when at last he flung the club with all his strength at the one on the left, it seemed to make no impression at all on the hard head of the enemy. Redoubling his efforts, he drew the wire tighter and tighter in his yellow teeth. In desperation, Randy suddenly

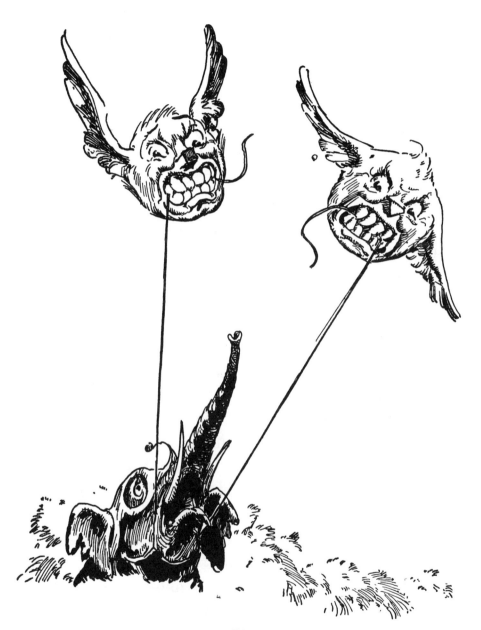

71

remembered the darts, and drawing one from the quiver, sent it speeding upward. The first missed, but as the Elegant Elephant began to sway and quiver beneath him, the second found its mark, striking the Headman squarely in the middle of the forehead. An expression of surprise and dismay overspread his wrinkled features, and next instant, with a terrific yawn, he dropped the wire and fell headlong to the rocks, where he rolled over and over and over.

"Great Goopers!" exclaimed Randy, hardly able to believe his luck. "Why, he's not hurt at all, but has fallen asleep."

"Watch the others, the—others!" gulped Kabumpo, shaking his head in an effort to free it from the wire. Already another had flown to take his fallen comrade's place, but before he could snatch the wire, Randy brought him to earth with one of his sharply pointed darts. The next who ventured he shot down too, and as the rest of the band came swarming down to see what was happening, Randy sent arrow after arrow winging into their midst till the flat, smooth rock was dotted with sleepy heads, for each one hit promptly fell asleep. Though his arm ached and his heart thumped uncomfortably,

Randy did not even pause for breath till he had sent the last arrow into the air, and then quite suddenly he realized he had won this strange and ridiculous battle. More than half of the ear-men, as he could not help calling them to himself, lay snoring on the ground; the rest with terrified shrieks and whistles were flapping off as fast as their ears would carry

them. Now entirely free of the wire, but still trembling and gasping, Kabumpo stared angrily after them.

"What I cannot understand," puffed Randy, sliding to the ground to examine a group of the enemy, "is what put them to sleep? I thought your darts might hurt or head them off or puncture them like balloons, but instead—here they are asleep, and

HOW asleep! Shall I pull out the arrows? I might need them later."

"They're not MY arrows," Kabumpo said, wrinkling his forehead in a puzzled frown. "I didn't have any arrows, but Ha, Ha, Kerumph!" The Elegant Elephant began to shake all over. "They must be Gaper Arrows—the Wakes must have stuck them in my pocket when they fetched my robe and headpiece. Pretty cute of the little rascals, at that. Why, these must be the same arrows the Winks shot at me, Randy, but my hide was too tough for them and they didn't work."

"Well, they certainly made short work of the Headmen," said Randy, turning one over gently with his foot. "Goodness! I thought you'd be choked and done for, old fellow!"

"Who, ME? Nonsense! My neck would have broken their teeth in another minute or two."

"Well, then, shall I pull out the arrows?" asked Randy, who had his own opinion about Kabumpo's narrow escape. "We could use them again some time."

"No, NO! Leave them in! So long as those arrows stick fast the little villains will sleep fast and that's the only way I can stand 'em."

"But suppose the others fly back?" Randy still hesitated.

"Pooh! Don't you worry about that." Kabumpo raised his trunk scornfully. "They're frightened out of their wits and probably half way to the Sapphire City by this time. And when they do come back, we won't be here."

"Won't we?" Dubiously Randy began to pace

across the bare and arid plateau. "I certainly don't think much of Headland, do you?"

"I wouldn't have it for a gift, even if they threw in a tusk brush and diamond earrings besides!" snorted Kabumpo. "Why, it's nothing but a humpy bumpy acre of rock without a tree, a house, a bird or even a blade of grass. I'd give the whole country for a mouthful of hay or a bucketful of water!"

"We might find a spring among the rocks," proposed Randy, hurrying along hopefully.

"More likely a fall," predicted Kabumpo, trudging gloomily behind him. But just then, Randy, who had vanished behind a sizable boulder, gave an excited whoop.

"Hi, yi, Kabumpo! We're here! We're here, right on the edge of it!" he shouted vociferously. "LOOK!" The Elegant Elephant, pushing round the rock, did look, then, mopping his forehead with the tip of his robe, sank heavily to his haunches and for a moment neither said a word. For, truly enough, the jagged point of Headland projected over the desert as a high cliff hangs over the sea. Below, the seething sand smoked, churned and tumbled, sending up sulphurous waves of heat that made both travelers cough and splutter.

"So, all we have to do is cross," gasped Randy, dashing the tears brought by the smoke out of his eyes.

"And a simple thing that will be," grunted the Elegant Elephant sarcastically, "seeing that one foot on the sand spells instant destruction. If we could just flap our ears like the Headmen, we could fly across."

"But as we can't," sighed Randy, seating himself despondently on a boulder. "What are we to do?"

"Well, that remains to be seen," muttered Kabumpo, who had not the faintest notion. " 'Never cross a Deadly Desert on an empty stomach,' is my motto, and I'm going to stick to it."

"Sticking to mottoes won't get us anywhere," Randy said, skimming a stone off the edge and watching with a little shudder as it was sucked down into the whirling sand. "Doesn't that desert make you thirsty? Goopers, if I had a dipperful of water I'd gladly do without the breakfast."

"Humph! looks as if you might have that wish." Feeling hurriedly in the right pocket of his robe, Kabumpo dragged out a waterproof as large as a tent. "Just spread this over me, will you?" he puffed anxiously. "Storm coming. Hear that thunder? Storm coming."

"Coming?" cried Randy, springing up to help Kabumpo with the buckles. "Why, it's here." He had to raise his voice to a scream to make himself heard above the gale that, arising apparently from nowhere, struck them furiously from behind. He had

77

just fastened the last strap of the waterproof to Kabumpo's left ankle when the rain swept down in perfect torrents; rain, accompanied by hailstones as big as Easter eggs. There was ample room for Randy beneath the Elegant Elephant, and standing between his front legs the young monarch lifted the waterproof, and reaching out caught a huge hail-

stone in his hand. Touching it against his parched lips, Randy gave a sigh of content, then crunching it up rapturously, stuck out his head and let the pelting downpour cool his hot and dusty face.

"Wonder if this will put out the desert?" he mused, ducking back as a terrible clap of thunder boomed like a cannon shot overhead. "SAY, it's a lucky thing you're so big, Kabumpo," he called up cheerily, "or we'd be blown away. Whee—listen to that wind, would you!"

"Have to do more than listen," howled the Elegant Elephant, bracing his feet and lowering his head. "Ahoy! below—catch hold of something, Randy! Help! Hi! Hold on! HOLD ON! For the love of blue—mountains! Here we GO! Here we blow! Oooomph! Bloomph! Ker—AHHHHH!"

"Oh, no, Kabumpo! NO!" Leaping up, Randy caught the Elegant Elephant's broad belt. "Put on —the brakes! Quick!" And Kabumpo did try making a futile stand against the tearing wind. But the mighty gale, whistling under his waterproof filled it up and out like a balloon, and with a regular ferry-boat blast, Kabumpo rose into the air and zoomed like a Zeppelin over the Deadly Desert, while Randy, hanging grimly to the strap of his belt, banged to and fro like the clapper on a bell.

CHAPTER 6

The Other Side of the Desert

REMEMBERING the deadly and destroying nature of the sands below, Randy did not dare to look down. Besides, holding on took all his strength and attention, for Kabumpo was borne like a leaf before the howling gale, faster and faster and faster, till he and Randy were too dazed and dizzy to know or care how far they had gone or where they were blowing to. Which was perhaps just as well, for, as suddenly as it had risen, the gale abated and, coasting down the last high hill of the wind, saved from a serious crash only by his faithful tarpaulin, which now acted as a parachute, Kabumpo came jolting to earth. With closed eyes and trunk held stiffly before him, the Elegant Elephant remained perfectly motionless awaiting destruction and wondering vaguely how it would feel. He was convinced that they had come down on the desert itself. Then, as no fierce blasts of heat assailed him, he ventured to open one eye. Randy, shaken loose by the force of the landing, had rolled to the ground a few feet away, and now, jumping to his feet, cried joyously:

"Why, it's over, Kabumpo—over, and so are we! Ho! I never knew you could fly, old Push-the-Foot."

"Neither did I," shuddered the Elegant Elephant, and jerking off the waterproof he flung it as hard and as far as he could.

"Oh, don't do that!" Randy dashed away to pick it up. "That good old coat saved our bacon and ballooned us across the desert as light as a couple of daisies."

"But we're no better off on this side than on the other," grumbled Kabumpo, surveying the barren countryside with positive hatred. "Not a house, a field, a farm or a castle in sight."

"The idea was to get away from castles, wasn't

it?" Randy grinned up at his huge friend and, folding the waterproof into a neat packet, tucked it back in its place.

"Well, there's one thing about castles," observed the Elegant Elephant, giving his robe a quick tug

here and there. "At least, the food's regular. I could eat a royal dinner from soup to napkins."

"Give me a boost up that tree and I'll have a look around," proposed Randy.

"Need a spy-glass to find anything worth looking at in this country," complained Kabumpo, lifting Randy into the fork of a gnarled old tree. Shinning expertly up the rough trunk, Randy looked carefully in all directions.

Chapter Six

"We certainly cleared the desert by a nice margin," he called down gaily. "It's at least a mile behind us, and toward the east I see a cluster of white towers that might be a castle."

"And nothing between," mourned Kabumpo with a hungry swallow. "No fields, orchards or melon patches?"

"There are fields, but they're too far away for me to see what's growing, and there's a forest too. What country is this, Kabumpo? Do you know?"

"Depends on how we blew," answered the Elegant Elephant, lifting Randy out of the tree and tossing him lightly over his shoulder. "If we blew straight from Headland, which is certainly the northwestern tip of the Gilliken Country of Oz, we should be in No Land. If we blew slantwise, this would be Ix."

"Then I hope we blew slantwise." Randy spread himself out luxuriantly behind Kabumpo's ears. "For if we are in Ix, we have only one country to cross before we reach Ev and Jinnicky's castle."

"And the sooner we start, the sooner we'll arrive," agreed Kabumpo, swinging into motion. "But if I drop in my tracks, boy, don't be too surprised. I'm hollow as a drum and weak as a violet."

"Too bad we're not like the Headmen," said

83

Randy, who felt dreadfully hollow himself. "Without a body, I suppose one does not feel hungry. Wonder what became of them, anyway?"

"Who cares?" sniffed Kabumpo, picking his way crossly through the rocks and brambles. "They probably blew about for a while, but with ears like sails, what's a gale of wind or weather? Ho! what's that I see yonder, a farmer?"

"No, just a hat stuck on a pole to scare away the crows," Randy told him after a careful squint. "But nothing grows in the field but rocks, so why do they bother?"

"Did you say a 'hat'?" Kabumpo's small eyes began to burn and twinkle, and breaking into a run he was across the field like a flash.

"Kabumpo!" gasped Randy, as the Elegant Elephant snatched the hat from the pole and took a huge bite from the brim. "Surely, surely you're not going to eat that old hat?"

"Why not?" demanded the Elegant Elephant, cramming the rest of the hat into his mouth and crunching it up with great gusto. "It's straw, isn't it? A little old and tough, to be sure, but nourishing, and anyway better than nothing!" Almost strangling on the crown, Kabumpo glanced sharply across the field, then looked apologetically back at his young rider. "Great Gooselberries," he muttered contritely, "I'm sorry as a goat. Why, I never saved you even an edge!"

"Oh, never mind," choked Randy, holding his sides at the very idea of such a thing. "Even if I were starving, I couldn't eat a hat. But look, old Push-

the-Foot, isn't that a barn showing over the top of that hill?"

"Barn!" wheezed Kabumpo, lifting his trunk joyfully. "Why, so it is! Ho! This is something like!" And hiccoughing excitedly, from the effects of the hat, no doubt, Kabumpo went galloping over the brow of the little hill.

85

A pleasant valley dotted with small farms stretched out below. Randy was relieved to note that its inhabitants were usual-looking beings like himself. Children rode gleefully on wagons piled high with hay. Farmers in wide-brimmed yellow hats, rather like those worn by the Winkies in Oz, worked placidly in the fields. Everyone seemed contented, calm and happy; that is, until Kabumpo, delighted to find himself again in a land of plenty, came charging down the hill trumpeting like a whole band of music.

"Oh, too bad, you've frightened them nearly out of their wits," mourned Randy, hanging on to Kabumpo's collar to keep his balance as the Elegant Elephant, forgetting his elegance, made a dash for the nearest hayrick.

"Help Hi—stop! Now see what you've done!"

To tell the truth, the havoc ensuing was not all Kabumpo's fault. No one in this tranquil valley of Ix had ever seen an elephant before, and the sight of one rushing down upon them was so unnerving and strange they fled in every direction, leaping into barns and houses, and barring and double-barring the doors against this terrifying monster. Horses hitched to their hay wagons cantered madly east and west, and the air was filled with loud shrieks, neighs and the bellows of stampeding cattle.

"Such dummies!" panted Kabumpo, coming to a complete standstill. "Well," he gave a tremendous sniff, "if they don't want to meet a King, a Prince and the most elegant elephant in Oz, what do we care? I've invited myself to breakfast anyhow, and

they can like it or Kabump it. Just wait till I load away one stack of this hay, my boy, and I'll find you a breakfast fit for a King and Traveler."

And the Elegant Elephant was good as his word. After tossing down a great mound of new-mown hay, he swaggered over to the nearest farmhouse. Pushing in the kitchen window with his trunk, he handed up to Randy everything the little farmer's wife had on her kitchen table—a bowl of milk, a pat of butter, a loaf of bread, a cold half chicken and three hard-boiled eggs.

"Do control yourself, madam," he advised, as the palpitating little lady flattened herself against the opposite wall. "These pearls will more than pay for your provisions."

Afraid to touch the lovely chain Kabumpo placed on the table, the little Ixey watched with round eyes as Kabumpo backed away.

"Ho, I guess that will give her something to tell her grandchildren!" snorted the Elegant Elephant. Randy was too busy taking rapturous bites, first of bread and then of chicken, to answer.

"Why is it that everything tastes so much better when you are traveling?" he remarked a bit later, as he finished off the rest of the chicken and put the bread, butter and eggs away for his lunch.

"'Cause we're hungrier, I suppose," smiled Kabumpo, crossing another field, "and then, there's the novelty."

Recalling the straw hat with a little chuckle, Kabumpo winked back at his young rider.

"But now that we've breakfasted I think we'd

better be moving. I see some of these farmers gathering up their courage and their pitchforks and I'm too full to fight."

"Pooh! they couldn't hurt us," boasted Randy, stretching out comfortably. "I rather wish they hadn't run off, though, I'd like to ask them something about the country, and you know, Kabumpo— I've never ridden on a hay wagon in all my life and I'd sorta like to try it."

"That's the worst of being a King," observed Kabumpo, walking carefully around a brown calf. "You miss a lot of the common and ordinary pleasures. Hmm—mmn, let's see, now, all the horses have run off, but there's still a heap of hay about—so why shouldn't you have a ride?"

"Without any wagon?" inquired Randy, looking wistfully at the largest of the haystacks.

"Why not?" puffed Kabumpo, and lifting Randy hurriedly down from his back, he rushed at the hayrick, burrowing into it with tusk, feet and trunk till he was in the exact center. Then heaving up with his back and forward with his trunk, he pushed till his head stuck out the other side. "Come ON!" he grunted triumphantly. "You'll not only have your hay ride, but I'll have my lunch!"

Throwing Randy to the top of the load, the Elegant Elephant, looking far from elegant, set off at a lumbersome gallop, carrying the haystack right along with him. At sight of his prize hayrick apparently running away by itself, the outraged owner stuck his head out of the window and screamed. But that did not bother Kabumpo. The load was but a

feather's weight to him, and with the young King of Regalia dancing and yelling on the top, he swept merrily through the startled valley.

Those at the lower end who had not seen Kabumpo arrive, now catching sight of a load of hay moving off by itself, simply fell against fences and barn doors, blinking and gulping with astonishment, too stunned and shocked to return the gay greetings of the nonchalant young Gilliken riding the load. Kabumpo, sampling stray wisps as he ran and peering out comically from under the hay, enjoyed to the utmost the sensation he was causing.

"Make a wish, my boy," he shouted exuberantly. "It's awfully lucky to wish on the first load of hay."

"Then I wish we would reach the Red Jinn's castle before night," decided Randy. "And wouldn't Jinnicky laugh if he could see us now? Did you leave a pearl for the hay, Kabumpo?"

"Certainly," retorted the elephant, speaking rather stuffily through the haystack. "We're travelers, not thieves. Hi! what's ahead, my lad? This load has shifted a bit over my left eye and I can scarcely see out of my right."

"A dry river bed," called Randy, bouncing up and down with the keenest enjoyment. "Go slow, old Push-the-Foot, or you'll lose your lunch."

"Not on your life!" puffed the Elegant Elephant. "I'll stop and eat it first. Ho—"

> "Hay foot, straw foot, any foot will do,
> Down the bank and up the bank, and now, how is
> the view?"

"Elegant," breathed Randy, grinning to himself

at Kabumpo's verses. "More fields—meadows—forests, everything!"

"But even so, I smell sulphur!" Kabumpo moved his trunk slowly from side to side. "Something's burning, my lad, and close at hand, too."

"Why, it's a HORSE!" Randy's voice cracked

from the sheer shock of the thing. "And coming straight for us, too. Wait! Stop! Hold on! No, maybe you'd better run. Great Gillikens, it's smoking!"

"A pipe?" inquired Kabumpo, trying to see through the fringe of hay that was obscuring his vision. "And what if it is? Am I, the Elegant Elephant of Oz, to run from a mere and miserable equine?"

"But this horse," squealed Randy, sliding head first off the haystack, "this horse is different. Oh, really, REALLY, Kabumpo, I think we'd better run."

"Never!" Pushing the hay off his forehead with his trunk, Kabumpo looked fiercely out, then, with a start that dislodged half the load, he began backing off as rapidly as he could, dragging Randy along by the tail of his coat.

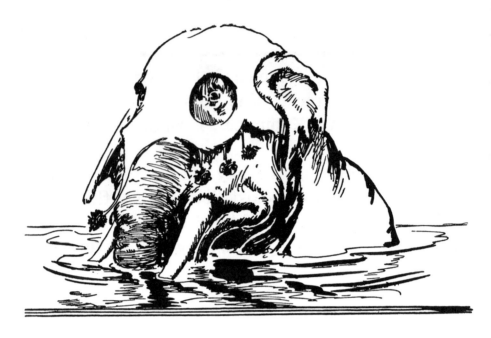

CHAPTER 7

The Princess of Anuther Planet

EVEN so, Kabumpo was not fast enough, and as the immense black charger with its tail and mane curling like smoke, its fiery nostrils flashing flames a foot long, came galloping upon them, Randy flung himself face down on the ground to escape its burning breath. The most terrifying thing about the black steed was the complete silentness of its coming. Its metal-shod feet struck the earth without making a sound, giving Kabumpo such a sense of unreality he could not believe it was true, nor move another step. In consequence, as the enor-

mous animal swirled to a halt before him, a dozen darting flames from its nostrils set fire to the load of hay on his back, enveloping him in a hot and exceedingly dangerous bonfire.

Now thoroughly aroused, Kabumpo leapt this way and that, and Randy, unmindful of his own danger, jumped up and tried to beat out the fire with his cloak. But the hay blazed and crackled and the Elegant Elephant would certainly have been roasted like a potato, had he not reared up on his hind legs and let the whole burning burden slide from his back. Scorched and infuriated, his royal robes burned and blackened, Kabumpo backed into a handy brook and sat down, from which position he glared with positive hatred at his prancing adversary. But a complete change had come over this strange and unbelievable steed; his nostrils no longer spurted flames and as Randy plumped down beside Kabumpo, deciding this was the safest spot for both of them, the lordly creature dropped to its knees and touched its forehead three times to the earth.

"Away, away! You big meddlesome menace!" panted the Elegant Elephant, throwing up his trunk. "Begone, you good-for-nothing hay burner!"

96

"But, Kabumpo," pleaded Randy, as the horse, paying no attention to the Elegant Elephant's angry screeches, began throwing little puffs of red smoke into the air, "he's trying to give us a message. LOOK!"

"Hail and salutations!" The words floated out smoothly and ranged themselves in a neat line. "I

hereby acknowledge you as my master! I can flash fire from the eye, the nose and the mouth; but you —you flash fire from the whole body! Hail and salutations from Thun, the Thunder Colt. Yonder rests my Mistress Planetty, Princess of Anuther Planet! Who are you, great-and-much-to-be-envied spurter of fire?"

"Sky writing!" gasped Randy. "Oh, Kabumpo,

how're we going to answer? He did not hear your scolding. I don't believe he can hear at all. Fire spurter! Ho, ho! And HOW are you going to keep up that reputation?"

"I'm not!" grunted Kabumpo, but in a much less savage voice, for he was almost completely won over by the Thunder Colt's flattery. "Hmmm-hhh, let me see, now, couldn't we signal to the silly brute? There he stands looking up in the air for an answer."

"Well," Randy said, "with your trunk and my arms we could form any number of letters, so—"

"This is Kabumpo, Elegant Elephant of Oz. I am Randy, King of Regalia."

With infinite pains and patience the two spelled out the message. Puzzled at first, then seeming to understand, Thun's clear yellow eyes snapped and twinkled with interest. Tossing his smoky mane, he puffed a single word into the air. "Come!" Then away he flashed at his noiseless gallop.

"Shall we?" cried Randy, jumping out of the creek, for he was curious to know more about the Thunder Colt and to meet the Princess of Anuther Planet. "Are you cooled off? Did the water put you out?"

"Oh, I'm put out all right," grumbled Kabumpo,

lurching up the bank. "Very put out and in splendid shape to meet a Princess, I must say."

"Come on, you don't look so bad," urged Randy, tugging impatiently at his tusk, while Kabumpo himself endeavored to wring the water out of his robe with his trunk. "Even without any trappings or jewels at all, you'd stand out in any company. There's nobody bigger or handsomer than you, Kabumpo! Know it?"

"HAH!" The Elegant Elephant let go his robe and gave Randy a quick embrace. "Then what are we waiting for, little Braggerwagger?"

Tossing the young monarch lightly over his shoulder, the Elegant Elephant started after the Thunder Colt, moving almost as smoothly and silently as Thun himself. Without one look behind, Thun had disappeared into a green forest, and how cool and delicious it seemed to Randy and Kabumpo after the dry desert lands they had been traversing. Flashing in and out between the tall trees, the Thunder Colt led them to an ancient oak, set by itself in a little clearing. Here, leaning thoughtfully against the bole of the tree, stood the little Princess of Anuther Planet.

Kabumpo, recognizing royalty at once when he

saw it, lifted his trunk in a grave and dignified salute. Randy bowed, but in such a daze of surprise and admiration he scarcely knew he was bowing. The small figure under the oak was strange and beautiful beyond description, giving an impression both of strength and delicacy. Planetty was fashioned of tiny meshed links, fine as the chain mail worn by medieval knights, of a metal that resembled silver, but which at the same time was iridescent and sparkling as glass. Yet the Princess of Anuther Planet was live and soft as Randy's own flesh-and-bone self. Her eyes were clear and yellow like Thun's; her hair, a cascade of gossamer net, sprayed out over her shoulders and fell half-way to her feet. Planetty's garments, trim and shaped to her figure, were of some veil-like net, and, floating from her shoulders, was a cloak of larger meshed metal thread almost like a fisherman's net.

"Highnesses, Highness! Oh, very high Highnesses!" Prancing lightly before her, Thun puffed his announcement importantly into the air. "Here you see Kabumpty, Nelegant Nelephant of Noz, and Sandy, King of Segalia."

"Oh, my goodness! He has us all mixed up," worried Randy in a whispered aside to Kabumpo, whose ears had gone straight back at the dreadful name Thun had fastened upon him.

"Never mind, I too am mixed up. Everything down here is too perfectly lettling."

"Oh, you can speak?" Leaning forward, Randy gazed delightedly down at the little metal maiden. He had been afraid at first she would use the same sky-writing talk as Thun.

"But surely," smiled Planetty, each word striking the air with the distinctness of a silver bell, so that Randy was almost as interested in the tune as in the sense. "Only the creature folk on Anuther Planet are without power of speech or sound making. They must go soft and silently. That is the lenith law."

"And a good law, too," observed Kabumpo, looking resentfully up at the Thunder Colt's fading message. "Permit me to introduce myself again. Your Highness, I am Kabumpo, Elegant Elephant of Oz, and this is Randy, King of Regalia, which is also in Oz."

"Oz?" marveled Planetty, lifting her spear-like silver staff, whose tip, ending in three metal links, fascinated Randy. "Is this, then, the Planet of Oz? And what are those, and these, and this?" In rapid succession the little Princess touched a cluster of violets growing round the base of the oak, a moss-covered rock and the tall tree itself.

"Why, flowers, rocks and a tree," laughed Randy. "Surely you must have flowers, trees and rocks on Anuther Planet."

"No, no, nothing like this—all these colors and shapes. Everything on my planet is flat and greyling." The metal maiden raised her hands, as she searched for the right words to explain Anuther Planet. "It is all so different with us," she confessed, dropping her arms to her side. "Yonder, we have zonitors; not trees, but tall shafts of metal to which we fasten our nets when we sleep or rest. Underfoot we have network of various sizes and thicknesses with here and there sprays of vanadium. In our vanadium springs we freshen and renew ourselves, and without them we stiffen and cease to move."

With one finger pressed to his forehead, Randy tried to visualize Planetty's strange greyling world, but Kabumpo, ever more practical, inquired sharply:

"And how often must you refresh and renew yourselves, Princess?"

"Every sonestor in the earling," answered the Princess with a bright nod.

Thun, tiring of a conversation he could not hear, had cantered off to investigate a rabbit, and Randy, sliding to the ground, came over to stand nearer to this strange little Princess.

"Kabumpo and I do not understand all those

words," he told her gently. " 'Sonestor—earling'—what do they mean?"

"Why, a sonestor," trilled Planetty, throwing back her head and showing all of her tiny silver teeth, "is one dark, one light, one dark, one light, one dark, one light, one dark, one light, one dark, one light, one dark, one light, one dark, one light, and earling is when you waken from ret."

"Help!" shuddered Kabumpo shaking his ears as if he had a bee in them.

"I know what she means," crowed Randy, snapping his fingers gleefully. "A sonestor on Anuther Planet is the same as a week here; all those lights and darks are days, and earling is the morning and ret is rest!"

"Then, do you realize," worried Kabumpo, as Planetty looked questioningly from one to the other, "that if this little lady and her colt are separated from their vanadium springs for a week, they will become stiff, motionless statues? And that—" the Elegant Elephant looked the pretty little Princess first up and then down. "That would be a great pity! We must help them back to Anuther Planet as soon as we can, my boy."

"Yes, yes, that is what you must do," Planetty

clapped her small silvery hands and blew a kiss to the elephant. "If Thun had just not jumped on that thunderbolt!"

"Jumped on a thunderbolt, did he?" A reluctant admiration crept into Kabumpo's voice. The Princess nodded so emphatically her long, lovely hair danced and shimmered round her face like a cloud shot with starlight.

"You see," she went on gravely, "we were on our way to a zorodell." Kabumpo and Randy exchanged startled glances, but, realizing there would be many odd words in Planetty's language, did not interrupt her. "And half-way there," continued Planetty calmly, "a dreaful storm overtook us. A bright flash of lightning frightened Thun, and though I signaled for him to stop, he sprang right up on a huge glowing thunderbolt that had fallen across the netway, and it fell and fell and fell—bringing us to where we now are."

"Well, that's one way of going places," commented Kabumpo, swinging his trunk from side to side.

"But how can we find Anuther Planet when none of us fly?" demanded Randy anxiously. "It must be miles above this country, for think how fast and far thunderbolts fall when they fall."

"Now you've forgotten the Red Jinn," boomed Kabumpo, winking meaningly at the young King, for at Randy's words the little Princess had covered her face with her hands and three yellow jewels had trickled through her fingers. "Jinnicky can help

Planetty and Thun go any place they wish," insisted Kabumpo in his loud challenging bass. "Come, Princess, summon your fire-breathing steed, and we will travel on to the most powerful wizard in Ev."

"Ev? Wizard? Oh, how gay it all sounds." Planetty's voice rang out merrily as Christmas bells. With a lively skip she tapped her staff three times on the ground, and Thun, though out of sight, came instantly bounding back to his little mistress. Vaulting easily upon his back, the Princess of Anuther Planet lifted her staff, and Kabumpo, picking up Randy, started away like a whole conquering army.

CHAPTER 8
On to Ev

I S there any way you can signal to your mount to trot ahead?" inquired Kabumpo, looking down sideways at the Thunder Colt, whose breath was blowing hot and uncomfortable against his side. "Let Thun be the vanguard," he suggested craftily. "When I trumpet once, turn him left; at two, turn right; at three, he must halt."

"Oh, fine," approved Planetty, tapping out the message with her heel on the Thunder Colt's flank. "That will be simply delishicus."

Thun evidently agreed with her, for, tossing his

112

smoky mane, he cantered to a position just ahead of the Elegant Elephant, at which Kabumpo heaved a huge sigh of relief. He did not wish to hurt Thun's feelings, neither did he wish to catch fire again.

"Here travel Thun, the Thunder Colt, Planetty, Princess of Anuther Planet; Kabumpty of Noz; and Slandy, King of Seegalia! Give way, all ye comers and goers, and arouse me not, for I am a seething mass of molten metal!"

"Is he really?" marveled Randy, gazing up at the fiery message floating like a banner over their heads. Planetty nodded absently, her interest so taken up with the wild flowers below, the blue sky above, and the wide-armed, lacy-leafed trees of this ancient forest she could not bear to turn her head for fear of missing something. On her own far-away metal planet, skies were grey and leaden, and the various levels of slate and silver strata arranged in stiff and net-like patterns. The gay colors of this bright new world simply delighted her, and Randy and Kabumpo she considered beings of rare and singular beauty. The word she used to herself when she thought of them was "netiful," which is Anuther way of saying beautiful.

"A wonder that high-talking Thomas couldn't get

a name straight once in a while!" complained Kabumpo out of one corner of his mouth, as Thun's sentence spiraled away in thin pink smoke.

"Oh, what difference does it make?" laughed Randy. "I think 'Kabumpty' is real cute."

"CUTE!" raged the Elegant Elephant with such a

fierce blast Planetty promptly turned Thun to the left.

"Now see what you've done," snickered Randy,

giving Kabumpo's ear a mischievous tweak. "They think you want them to go left."

"As a matter of fact, I do," snapped Kabumpo grumpily. "We must go east through Ix and then north to Ev."

"Puzzling and more puzzling," murmured Planetty, looking round at the Elegant Elephant. "Where are all these curious places, Bumpo dear? I thought all the time we were in Noz. Did you not tell us you were the Big Bumpo of Noz?"

Randy peered rather anxiously over Kabumpo's ear to see how he was taking this second nickname, but he need not have worried. The "dear Bumpo," spoken in the metal maid's ringing tones, fell like a charm on Kabumpo's ruffled feelings. And, fairly oozing complacency and importance, he began to explain his own and Randy's real names and countries, hoping Planetty would straighten them out in her own head, if not in Thun's.

"You are right," he started off sonorously. "Randy and I both live in the Land of Oz, a great oblong country entirely surrounded by a desert of burning sand. But in Oz there are many, many Kingdoms: first of all, the four large realms, the Gilliken Country of the North, the Quadling Country of the South, the Empire of the Winkies in the East, and the Land of the Munchkins in the West. Each of these Kingdoms has its own sovereign; but all are under the supreme rule of Ozma, a fairy Princess as lovely as your own small self, and Ozma lives in an Emerald City in the exact center of Oz."

Kabumpo paused impressively while Planetty's eyes twinkled merrily at his delicate flattery. "Now Randy and I hail from the north Gilliken Country of Oz," proceeded the Elegant Elephant, moving along as he spoke in a grand and leisurely manner. "I come from the Kingdom of Pumperdink, and Randy from the Regal little realm of Regalia. Only yesterday I arrived in Regalia to visit Randy, and we are now on our way to the castle of the Red Jinn, as I think I told you before. If we were in Oz, my dear—" Kabumpo rather lingered over the "dear"— "Ozma and her clever assistant, the Wizard of Oz, would quickly transport you to Anuther Planet with the magic belt. But, you see, we are not in Oz, for the same storm that overtook you and Thun overtook us, and hurled us across the Deadly Desert to this Kingdom of Ix, where we all now find ourselves. Fortunately, too, for otherwise we might never have met a Princess from Anuther Planet."

116

Chapter Eight

The little Princess nodded in bright agreement.

"So—" continued Kabumpo, picking a huge tiger-lily and holding it out to her, "as it is too difficult to travel back to the Emerald City of Oz, we will take you with us to the Wizard of Ev, whose castle is on the Nonestic Ocean in the country adjoining Ix."

"And a wizard is what?" Planetty turned almost completely round on her black charger, smiling teasingly over the tiger-lily at Kabumpo.

"Why, a wizard—er—a wizard—" The Elegant Elephant fumbled a bit trying to find the right words to explain.

"A wizard is a person who can do by magic what other people cannot do at all," finished Randy neatly.

"Magic?" Planetty still looked puzzled.

"Oh, never mind all the words," comforted Kabumpo, flapping his ears good naturedly, "you'll soon see for yourself what they all mean, and I'm sure Jinnicky will be charmed to do his best tricks for you and send you back in fine and proper style to your own planet."

"Yes, Jinnicky can do almost anything," boasted Randy, taking off his crown and setting it back very much atilt, "and he's good fun too. You'll like Jinnicky."

"As much as Big Bumpo?" Planetty rolled her soft eyes fondly back at the Elegant Elephant, and Randy, feeling an unaccountable twinge of jealousy, wished she would look at him that way.

"Oh, maybe not so much as Kabumpo; of course,

there's nobody like HIM—but pretty much as much," declared the young King loyally.

"But I like everything down here," decided Planetty, leaning forward to tickle Thun's ear with the lily. "It's all so nite and netiful."

"So now we know what we are," whispered Randy under his breath to Kabumpo. "And wait till Jinnicky sees us traveling with a fire-breathing Thunder Colt and the Princess of Anuther Planet. Oh, don't we meet important people on our journeys, Kabumpo?"

"Well, don't they meet US?" murmured the Elegant Elephant, increasing his speed a little to keep up with Thun. "Though I wouldn't call this colt important myself. How is he any better than an ordinary horse? His breath is hot and dangerous,

and it's not much fun traveling with a deaf and dumb brute who burns everything he breathes on."

"Oh, he's not so dumb," observed Randy. "Look at the way he leaped over that fallen log just now, and think how useful he'll be at night to blaze a trail and light the camp fires."

"Hadn't thought of that," admitted Kabumpo grudgingly. "I guess he would show up pretty well in the dark, and I suppose that does make him trail

119

blazer and lighter of the fires for this particular expedition. Ho, HO! KERUMPH! And between you and me and the desert, this expedition had better move pretty fast and not stop for sightseeing. Suppose these two Nuthers had that vanadium shower at the beginning of the week instead of the middle, that would give them only about two more days to go? Great Goosefeathers! I'd hate to have 'em stiffen up on us half-way to Jinnicky's. I might carry the Princess, but what would we do with the colt?"

"Let's not even think of it," begged Randy with a little shudder. "Great Goopers! Kabumpo, I hope Jinnicky will be at home and his magic in good working order and powerful enough to send them back or keep them here if they decide to stay."

"If they decide to stay?" Kabumpo looked sharply back at his young rider. "Why should they?"

"Well, Planetty said she liked it down here, you heard her yourself a moment ago, and I thought maybe—" Randy's face grew rosy with embarrassment.

"Ha, Ha! So that's the way the wind lies!" Kabumpo chuckled soundlessly. "Well, I wouldn't count on it, my lad," he called up softly. "She probably

has some nite Planetty Prince waiting for her up
yonder, and will fly away without so much as a backward glance. And as for Jinnicky being at home—
why shouldn't he be at home? And as for his magic
not being powerful enough—why shouldn't it be

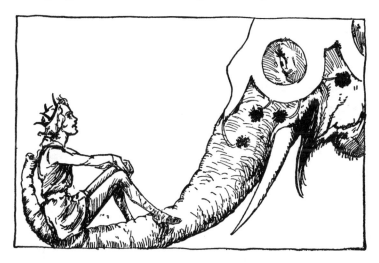

powerful enough? He was in fine shape and form
when I saw him in the Emerald City three years ago.
By the way, why weren't you at that grand celebration? I understood Ozma invited all the Rulers of
the Realm."

"Uncle Hoochafoo did not want me to leave,"
sighed Randy. "He thinks a King's place is in his
castle."

"I wonder what he thinks now?" said Kabumpo,

trumpeting three times, for Thun was racing along too far ahead of them.

"Probably has all the wise men and guards running in circles to find me," giggled Randy, immediately restored to good humor. "And say, when I do get back, old Push-the-Foot, I'M going to be KING and everything will be very different and gay. Yes, there'll be a lot of changes in Regalia," he decided, shaking his head positively. "Why, all those dull receptions and reviewings would tire a visitor to tears."

"Ho, Ho! So you're still expecting her to visit you?" Waving his trunk, Kabumpo called out in a louder voice. "Not so fast there, Princess; hold Thun back a bit. We might run into danger and we should all keep together on a journey. Besides," Kabumpo cleared his throat apologetically, "Randy and I must stop for a bite to eat."

Planetty's eyes widened, as they always did at strange words and customs, but she tugged obediently at Thun's mane and the Thunder Colt came to an instant halt. Randy himself tried to coax the little Princess to eat something, but she was so upset and puzzled by the idea, he finally desisted and tried to share his bread and eggs with Kabumpo. But the

Elegant Elephant generously refused a morsel, knowing Randy had little enough for himself, and lunched as best he could from the shoots of young trees and saplings. Thun was so interested when Kabumpo quenched his thirst at a small spring that he too thrust his head into the bubbling waters, but withdrew it instantly and with such an expression of pain and distress Randy concluded that water hurt the Thunder Colt as much as fire hurt them.

He was quite worried till the flames began to spurt from Thun's nostrils, for he was afraid the water might have put out Thun's fire and hastened the time when he should lose all power of life and motion.

"Do you do this often?" inquired Planetty, as Randy tucked what was left into one of Kabumpo's small pockets.

"Eat?" Randy laughed in spite of himself. "Oh,

about three times a day—or light," he corrected himself hastily, remembering Planetty had so designated the daytime. "I suppose that vanadium spray or shower keeps you and Thun going, the way food does Kabumpo and me?"

Planetty nodded dreamily, then, seeing Kabumpo was ready to start, she tapped Thun with her silver heels and away streaked the Thunder Colt, Kabumpo swinging along at a grand gallop behind him.

"Strange we have not passed any woodsmen's huts, nor seen any wild animals," called Randy, jamming his crown down a little tighter to keep it from sailing off. "Hi! Watch out, there old Push-a-Foot! There's a wall ahead stretching away on all sides and going up higher than higher. What's a wall doing in a forest? Perhaps it shuts in the private shooting preserve of Queen Zixie herself. Say—ay— I'd like to meet the Queen of this country, wouldn't you?"

"No time, no time," puffed the Elegant Elephant, giving three short trumpets to warn Planetty to halt Thun. "Great Grump! whoever built this wall wanted to shut out everything, even the sky. Can't even get a squint of the top, can you?"

"Is this the great Kingdom of Ev?" asked Planetty, who had pulled Thun up short and was looking at the wooden wall with lively interest.

"No, no, we're not nearly to Ev." The Elegant Elephant shook his head impatiently. "Back of this wall lives someone who dotes on privacy, I take it,

or why should he shut himself in and everyone else out? Now, then, shall we cruise round or knock a hole in the wood? I don't see any door, do you, Randy?"

"No, I don't." Standing on the elephant's back, Randy examined the wall with great care. "Why, it goes for miles," he groaned dolefully. "Miles!"

"Then we'll just bump through." Backing off, Kabumpo lowered his head and was about to lunge for-

126

ward when Randy gave his ear a sharp tweak.

"Look!" he directed breathlessly. "Look!" While they had been talking, Thun had been sniffing curiously at the wooden wall and now a whole round section of it was blazing merrily. "Hurray! He's burned a hole big enough for us all to go through," yelled the young King gleefully. "Come ON!"

Vexed to think the Thunder Colt had solved the difficulty so easily, and worried lest the whole wall should catch fire, Kabumpo signaled for Planetty to precede him. But he need not have worried about Thun's firing the wall. The Thunder Colt had burned as neat a hole in the boards as a cigarette burns in paper, and while the edges glowed a bit, they soon smouldered out, leaving a huge circular opening. So, without further delay, Kabumpo stepped through, only to find himself facing the most curious company he had seen in the whole course of his travels.

CHAPTER 9
The Box Wood

WHY! Why, they're all in boxes!" breathed Randy, as a group with upraised and boxed fists advanced upon the newcomers.

"Chillywalla! Chillywalla!" yelled the Boxers, their voices coming muffled and strange through the hat-boxes they wore on their heads.

"Chillywalla, Chillywalla, Chillywalla!" echoed Planetty, waving cheerfully at the oncoming host.

"Shh-hh, pss-st, Princess, that may be a war cry," warned Randy, drawing his sword and swinging it so swiftly round his head it whistled. Thun, too as-

128

tonished to move a step, stood with lowered head, his flaming breath darting harmlessly into the moist floor of the forest.

"Chillywalla! Chillywalla! Chillywalla!" roared the Boxers, keeping a safe distance from Kabumpo's lashing trunk. "Chillywalla! CHILLYWALLA!" Their voices rose loud and imploring. As Randy slid off the Elegant Elephant's back to place himself beside Planetty, a perfectly enormous Boxer came clumping out of the Box Wood to the left.

"Yes! Yes?" he grunted, holding on his hat-box as he ran. When he caught sight of the travelers, he stopped short, and, not satisfied with peering through the eyeholes in his hat-box, took it off altogether and stood staring at them, his square eyes almost popping from his square head. "Box their ears, box their ears! Box their heads and arms and rears! Box their legs, their hands and chests, box that fire plug 'fore all the rest! An IRON box!" screamed Chillywalla, as Thun, with a soundless snort, sent a shower of sparks into a candy box bush, toasting all the marshmallows in the boxes. "Oh, aren't you afraid to go about in this barebacked, barefaced, unboxed condition?" he panted, "exposed to the awful dangers of the raw outer air?"

Chillywalla hastily clapped on his hat box, but not before Randy noticed that his ears were nicely boxed, too. Without waiting for an answer to his question, the Boxer, with one shove of his enormous boxed fist, pushed Thun under a Box Tree. Planetty had just time to leap from his back when Chillywalla shook a huge iron box loose and it came clanking down over the Thunder Colt. It was open at the bottom, and Thun, kicking and rearing underneath, jerked it east and west.

"He'll soon grow used to it," muttered Chillywalla, jabbing a dozen holes in the metal with a sharp pick he had drawn from a pocket in his box coat. "Now, then, who's next? Ah! What a lovely lady!" Chillywalla gazed rapturously at the Princess from Anuther Planet, then clapping his hands, called sharply: "Bring the jewel boxes for her ears, flower boxes for herself, a bonnet box for her head, candy boxes for her hands, slipper boxes for those tiny silver feet. Bring stocking boxes, glove boxes, and hurry! HURRY!"

"Oh, PLEASE!" Randy put himself firmly between Planetty and the determined Chillywalla. "The outer air does not hurt us at all, Mister Chillywalla; in fact, we like it!"

130

"Just try to find a box big enough for me!" invited Kabumpo, snatching up the little Princess and setting her high on his shoulder.

"I think I have a packing box that would just fit,"

131

mused the Chief Boxer, folding his arms and looking sideways at the Elegant Elephant.

"Pack him up, pack him off, send him packing!" chattered the other Boxers, who had never seen anything like Kabumpo in their lives and distrusted him highly. But Chillywalla himself was quite interested in his singular visitors and inclined to be more than friendly.

"Better try our boxes," he urged seriously, as he took the pile of bright cardboard containers an assistant had brought him. "Without bragging, I can say that they are the best boxes grown—stylish, nicely fitting and decidedly comfortable to wear."

"Ha, ha!" rumbled Kabumpo, rocking backward and forward at the very idea. "Mean to tell me you wear boxes over your other clothes and everywhere you go?"

"Certainly." Chillywalla nodded vigorously. "Do you suppose we want to stand around and disintegrate? What happens to articles after they are taken out of their boxes?" he demanded argumentatively. "Tell me that."

"Why," said Randy, thoughtfully, "they're worn, or sold, or eaten, or spoiled—"

"Exactly." Chillywalla snapped him up quickly.

132

"They are worn out; they lose their freshness and their newness. Well, we intend to save ourselves from such a fate, and we do," he added complacently.

"You're certainly fresh enough," chuckled Kabumpo with a wink at Randy.

"But might not these boxes be fun to wear?" inquired Planetty, looking rather wistfully at the bright heap the Boxer Chief had intended for her.

"No, No and NO!" rumbled Kabumpo positively. "No boxes!"

"As you wish." Chillywalla shrugged his shoulders under his cardboard clothes box. "Shall I unbox the horse?"

"Better not," decided Randy, looking anxiously at the sparks issuing from the punctures in Thun's box. "But perhaps you would show us the way through this—this—"

"Box Wood," finished Chillywalla. "Yes, I will be most honored to conduct you through our forest. And you may pick as many boxes as you wish, too," he added generously. "I'd like to do something for people who are so soon to spoil and wither."

"Ha, ha! Now, I'm sure that's very kind of you," roared Kabumpo, wiping his eyes on the fringe of his robe. "And I think it best we hurry along, my good

133

fellow. Ho, whither away? It would never do to have a spoiled King and Princess and a bad horse and elephant on your hands."

"Oh, if you'd ONLY wear our boxes!" begged Chillywalla, almost ready to cry at the prospect of his

visitors spoiling on the premises. Then as Kabumpo shook his head again, the Big Boxer started off at a rapid shuffle, anxious to have them out of the woods as soon as possible. Thun, during all this conversation, had been kicking and bucking under his iron box, but now Planetty tapped out a reassuring message with her staff and the Thunder Colt quieted down. On the whole, he behaved rather well, following the signals his little mistress tapped out, and pushing the iron box along without too much discomfort or complaint, though occasional indignant and fiery protests came puffing out of his iron container.

Randy considered the journey through the Box Wood one of their gayest and most entertaining adventures. The woodmen, in their brightly decorated boxes, shuffled cheerfully along beside them, stopping now and then to point with pride to their square box-like dwellings set at regular intervals under the spreading boxwood trees. The whole forest was covered by an enormous wooden box that shut out the sky and gave everything an artificial and unreal look. It was in one side of this monster box that Thun had burned the hole to admit them. Randy and Planetty, riding sociably together on Kabumpo's back, picked boxes from branches of all the trees they could reach, and it was such fun and so exciting they paid scarcely any attention to the remarks of Chillywalla. Even the Elegant Elephant snapped off a box or two and handed them back to his royal riders.

"Oh, look!" exulted Randy, opening a bright blue cardboard box. "This is just full of chocolate candy."

"Oh, throw that trash away," advised Chillywalla contemptuously. "We think nothing of the stuff that

grows inside, it's the boxes themselves we are after."

"But this candy is good," objected Randy after sampling several pieces. "And mind you, Kabumpo, Planetty has just picked a jewel box full of real chains, rings and bracelets."

"Oh, they are netiful, netiful," crooned the Princess of Anuther Planet, hugging the velvet jewel box to her breast.

"Keep them if you wish," sniffed Chillywalla, "but they're just rubbish to us. When we pick boxes we toss the contents away."

"Now, that's plain foolishness," snorted Kabumpo, aghast at such a waste, as Randy picked a pencil box full of neatly sharpened pencils and Planetty a tidy sewing kit fitted out with scissors, needles and spools of thread. The thimble was not quite ripe, but as Planetty had never stitched a stitch in her royal life, she did not notice nor care about that. Indeed, before they came to the other side of the Box Wood, she and Randy were sitting in the midst of a high heap of their treasures, and Kabumpo looked as if he were making a lengthy safari, loaded up and down for the journey.

Randy had stuffed most of the boxes into big net bags Kabumpo always brought along for emergencies, and these he tied to the Elegant Elephant's harness. There were bread boxes packed with tiny loaves and biscuits, cake boxes stuffed with sugar buns and cookies, stamp boxes, flower boxes, glove boxes, coat and suit boxes. Last of all, Randy picked a Band Box and it played such gay tunes when he

lifted the lid, Planetty clapped her silver hands, and even Kabumpo began to hum under his breath. Traveling through the Box Wood with kind-hearted Chillywalla was more like a surprise party than anything else. To Planetty it was all so delightful, she began to wonder how she had ever been satisfied with her life on Anuther Planet.

"Are all the countries down here as different and

happy as this?" she asked, fingering the necklace she had taken from the jewel box. "All our countries are greyling and sad. No birds sing, no flowers grow, and people are all the same."

"Oh, just wait till you've been to OZ," exclaimed Randy, shutting the band box so he could talk better. "Oz countries are even more surprising than this, and wait till you've seen Ev and Jinnicky's Red Glass Castle!"

"You'll never reach it," predicted Chillywalla, shaking his hat box gloomily. "You'll spoil in a few hours now, especially the big one, loaded down with all that stuff and rubbish. Throw it away," he begged again, looking so sorrowful Randy was afraid he was going to burst out crying. "Toss out that rubbish and wear our boxes before it is too late!"

"Rubbish!" Randy shook his finger reprovingly at the Boxer. "Why, all these things are terribly nice and useful. If we go through enemy countries, we can placate the natives with cakes and cigars, and if we go through friendly countries, we'll use the suits and flowers and candy for gifts. Really, you've been a great help to us, Mr. Chillywalla, and if you ever come to Regalia, you may have anything in my castle you wish!"

"Are there any boxes in your castle?" Chillywalla peered up at Randy through the slits in his hat box.

"Not many," admitted Randy truthfully. "You see, in my country we keep the contents and throw the boxes away."

"Throw the boxes away!" gasped Chillywalla, jumping three times into the air. "Oh, you rogues!

You rascals! You—YOU BOXIBALS! Lefters! Righters! Boxers all! Here! Here at once! Have at these Box-destroying savages!"

"Now see what you've done," mourned Kabumpo, as hundreds of the Boxers, heeding Chillywalla's call, darted out of their dwellings and came leaping from behind the box bushes and trees. "You've started a war! That's what!"

"Box them! Box them good!" shrieked Chillywalla,

raining harmless blows on Kabumpo's trunk with his boxed fists. A hundred more boxed both Thun and the Elegant Elephant from the rear, and so loud and angry were their cries Planetty covered her ears.

"Too bad we have to leave when everything was so pleasant," wheezed Kabumpo. "But never mind, here's the other side of the Box Wood. Flatten out, youngsters, and I'll bump through."

And bump through he did, with such a splintering of boards it sounded like an explosion of cannon crackers. Thun, at three taps from Planetty, bumped after him, and before the Boxers realized what was happening they were far away from there.

"I'll soon have that box off you!" panted Kabumpo. And putting his trunk under Thun's iron box, he heaved it up in short order, screaming shrilly as he did, for the Thunder Colt's breath had made the metal uncomfortably hot.

"I thank you, great and mighty Master!" Thun sent the words up in a perfect shower of sparks. "Let us begone from these noxious boxers."

"Oh, they're not so bad," mused Randy, as Planetty signaled for Thun to go left. "Just peculiar. Imagine keeping the boxes and throwing away all the lovely things inside. And imagine a country where everything grows in boxes!" he added, standing up to wave at Chillywalla and his square-headed comrades, who were looking angrily through the break in the side of their wall.

"Good-bye!" he called clearly. "Good-bye, Chilly-walla, and thanks for the presents!"

"Boxibals!" hissed the Boxer Chief and his men,

shaking their fists furiously at the departing visitors.

"And that makes us no better than cannibals, I suppose," grunted Kabumpo, looking rather wearily at the stretch of forest ahead. He had rather hoped to find himself in open country.

CHAPTER 10

Night in the Forest

ALL afternoon the four travelers moved through the Ixian forest, Planetty exclaiming over the flowers, ferns and bright birds that flitted from tree to tree, Thun sending up frequent high-flown sentences, Kabumpo and Randy looking rather anxiously for some landmark that would prove they were on the road to Ev. As it grew darker the Elegant Elephant wisely decided to make camp, stopping in a small, tidy clearing for that purpose. As Kabumpo swung to an impressive halt, Randy slid to the ground, pulling the net bags with him, and began to sort out the boxes containing food. Then he quickly gathered some faggots for a fire, as the night was raw and chilly, and had Planetty signal Thun to breathe on the wood. Thun, only too happy to be of some use, quickly lighted the camp fire and he and the little Princess watched curiously while Randy prepared his own and Kabumpo's supper, making coffee in a tin box with some water Kabumpo had fetched in his collapsible canvas bucket. The Elegant Elephant did rather well with the contents of seven cake boxes and four bread and cereal containers, and Randy found so many good things to eat among Chillywalla's presents he felt sorry not to be able to share them with Planetty or Thun.

"It would be more fun if you ate too," he observed, looking down sideways at the little Princess, who was sitting on a boulder, hands clasped about her knees, while she gazed contentedly up at the stars.

"Would it?" Planetty smiled faintly, tapping her silver heels against the rock. "This seems nite enough," she sighed, stretching up her arms luxuriantly, "but now it is time to ret."

Slipping off her long metal cape, the Princess of Anuther Planet tossed one end against a white birch and the other to a tall pine. To Randy's surprise the

ends of the cape instantly attached themselves to the trees, making a soft flexible hammock. Into this Planetty climbed with utmost ease and satisfaction.

"Good net, Randy and Big Bumpo, dear," she called softly. "Take care of Thun. I've told him to stay where he is till the earling, and he will, he will."

With a smile Planetty closed her bright eyes and

the wind swaying her silver hammock soon rocked her to sleep. It had been a long day and Randy felt very drowsy himself. Walking over to the Thunder Colt, he turned his head so that his fiery breath would fall harmlessly on a cluster of damp rocks. He was pleased to find this steed from another planet so obedient and gentle. Though formed of some live

145

and lively black metal, Thun was soft and satiny to the touch and seemed to enjoy having his ears scratched and his neck rubbed as much as an ordinary horse.

"Tap me twice on the shoulder if aught occurs, Slandy," he signaled, blowing the words out lazily between Randy's pats. "And good net to you, my Nozzies! Good net!"

"That language is just full of foolishness," sniffed Kabumpo, spreading a blanket on the ground for Randy, and then stretching himself full length beneath a beech tree. "Put out the fire, Nozzy, my lad, the creature's breath makes light enough to frighten off any wild men or monsters."

"Oh, I don't believe there are any wild beasts or savages in this forest," Randy said, stamping out the embers of the camp fire. "It's too quiet and peaceful. I have an idea we're almost across Ix and will reach Ev by morning. What do you think, Kabumpo?"

Kabumpo made no answer, for the Elegant Elephant had stopped thinking and was already comfortably asnore. So, with a terrific yawn, Randy wrapped himself in the blanket and, curling up close to his big and faithful comrade, fell into an instant and pleasant slumber. Morning came all too soon, and Randy was rudely awakened by Kabumpo, who was shaking him violently by the shoulders.

"Come on! Come on!" blustered the Elegant Elephant impatiently. "Stir out of it, my boy, we've all been up for hours. Is it proper to lie abed and let a Princess light the fire?"

"She didn't!" Sitting bolt upright, Randy saw that

Planetty, with Thun's help, actually had lighted a fire and set water to boil in the tin box just as he had done the evening before.

"Oh, my goodness, goodness, Planetty! You mustn't do that rough work," he exclaimed, hurrying over to take the big cake box from Planetty's hands.

"Why not?" beamed the little Princess, hugging

147

the box close. "See, I have found the great choconut cake for Big Bumpo to eat—I mean neat."

"Ha, ha! Choconut cake!" Kabumpo swayed merrily from side to side. "Very neat, my dear. If there's one thing I love for breakfast it's choconut cake." Laughing so he could hardly keep his balance, Kabumpo held out his trunk for the cake box. "What a splendid little castle keeper you'll make for some young King, Netty, my child!"

"Netty? Is that now my name?" Planetty pushed back her flying cloud of hair with an interested sniff.

"If you like it," said Randy, his ears turning quite red at Kabumpo's teasing remarks. Leading the little Princess to a flat rock, he sat her down with great ceremony and then began opening up boxes of crackers and fruit.

"Netty's a nite name," decided the Princess, her head thoughtfully on one side. "I must tell Thun."

Skipping over to the Thunder Colt, who with drooping head and tail was enjoying a little colt nap, she tapped out her new nickname in the strange code she used when talking to him.

"No longer Planetty of Anuther Planet!" flashed Thun, awake in a twinkling and sending up his message in a shower of sparks. "But Anetty of Oz!"

"At least he's left off the N." mumbled Kabumpo, speaking thickly through the cocoanut cake which he had tossed whole into his capacious mouth. "Sounds rather well, don't you think?"

"Wonderful!" agreed Randy, who could scarcely keep his eyes off the sparkling little Princess. "It's too bad she's not like us, Kabumpo, then she could go back to Oz and stay there always."

"If she were like us, she wouldn't be so interesting," said Kabumpo, shaking his head judiciously. "Besides, down here the poor child is completely out of her element and liable to disintegrate or suffocate or Ev knows what—" he went on, discarding a box of prunes for a carton of tea.

"How was the cake?" Randy changed the subject, for he could not bear to think of Planetty in danger of any sort.

"Stale," announced Kabumpo, making a wry face as he swallowed some tea leaves. "I'll certainly be glad to catch up with some regular elephant food. This eating bits out of boxes is diabolical—simply diabolical! Here, give me those crackers and eat some of that other stuff. And look at little Netty Ann, would you, shaking out that blanket as if she'd

been traveling with us for years. Why, the lass is a born housewife!"

"And isn't she pretty?" smiled Randy, waving to Planetty as he began packing the boxes in the net bags again and stamping out the fire. "I wonder what it's like up where she lives, Kabumpo?"

"Why not ask her?" Swinging up his saddle sacks, Kabumpo called gaily to the little Princess, who came running over, the blanket neatly folded on her arm.

"Thank you, Netty. You are certainly a great help to us!" Taking the blanket and giving her an approving pat on the shoulder, Randy caught hold of Kabumpo's belt strap and pulled himself easily aloft. "All ready to go?"

Planetty nodded cheerfully as she mounted the Thunder Colt.

"Will this lightling be as nite as the last?" she demanded, tapping Thun gently with her staff.

"Nicer," promised Randy as Thun pranced merrily ahead, Planetty's long cape billowing like a silver cloud behind them.

"What do you do when you are at home?" called Randy as Kabumpo, giving two short trumpets, followed close on the heels of the Thunder Colt.

"Home?" Planetty turned a frankly puzzled face.

"I mean, do you have a house or a castle?" persisted Randy, determined to have the matter settled in his mind once for all. "Do you have brothers and sisters, and is your father a King?"

"No house, no castle, no those other words," answered Planetty in even greater bewilderment. "On Anuther Planet each is to herself or himself alone. One floats, rides, skips or drifts through the leadling heights and lowlands, hanging the cape where one happens to be."

"Regular gypsies," murmured Kabumpo under his breath. "So nobody belongs to nobody, and nobody has anybody? Sounds kind of crazy to me."

"Yes, if you have no families, no fathers or mothers—" Randy was plainly distressed by such a country and existence—"I don't see how you came to be at all."

"We rise full grown from our Vanadium springs, and naturally I have my own spring. Is that, then, my father?"

"Tell her 'yes,'" hissed Kabumpo between his tusks. "Why mix her all up with our way of doing things? If she wants a spring for a father, let her have it!" Kabumpo waved his trunk largely. "Ho, ho, kerumph! I've always thought of springs as a cure for rheumatism, but live and learn—eh, Randy —live and learn."

Randy paid small attention to the Elegant Elephant's asides; he was too busy explaining life as it was lived in Oz to Planetty, making it all so bright and fascinating, the eyes of the little Princess fairly sparkled with interest and envy.

"I think I will not go with you to this Wizard of Ev," she announced in a small voice as the young

King paused for breath. "I do not believe I shall like that old wizard or his castle."

Touching Thun with her staff, Planetty turned the Thunder Colt sideways and went zigzagging so rapidly through the trees they almost lost sight of her entirely.

"Now what?" stormed the Elegant Elephant, charging recklessly after her through the forest. "What's come over the little netwit? Come back!

153

Come back, you foolish girl!" he trumpeted anxiously. "We'll take you to Oz after you've been to Ev," he added with a sudden burst of comprehension.

At Kabumpo's promise, Planetty half turned on her charger. "But this Wizard of Ev will send us back to Anuther Planet. It is yourself that has said so."

"No, no! We just said he would help you!" shouted Randy, leaning forward and waving both arms for Planetty to turn back. "Oh, you really must see Jinnicky," he begged earnestly. "Without his magic you cannot live away from that Vanadium spring. Do you want to be stiff and still as a statue for the rest of your days?"

"I'd rather be a statue down here with you and Bumpo, where the birds sing and the flowers grow and the woods are green and wonderful, than to be a live Princess of Anuther Planet!" sighed the metal maiden, hiding her face in Thun's mane.

"You WOULD?" cried Randy, almost falling off the elephant in his extreme joy and excitement. "Then you just SHALL, and Jinnicky will change everything so you can live down here always and come back to Oz with Kabumpo and me! Would you like that, Planetty?"

"Oh, that would be netiful!" Clasping Thun with both arms, the little Princess laid her soft cheek against his neck. "NETIFUL!"

"Then ride on, Princess! Ride on!" Kabumpo spoke gruffly, for his feelings had quite overcome him. "Toss me a 'kerchief, will you, Randy?" he

gulped desperately. "Oh, boo hoo, kerSNIFF! To think she really likes us that much! Do you think she'd hear if I blew my trunk?"

"No, no, she's way ahead of us now," whispered Randy, handing an enormous handkerchief down to Kabumpo after taking a sly wipe on it himself. "Oh, isn't this a gorgeous day, Kabumpo, and isn't everything turning out splendidly? And see there—we've actually come to the end of the forest."

CHAPTER 11

The Field of Feathers

GOOD Gapers, everything's pink!" marveled Randy as Kabumpo, still muttering and snuffling, pushed his way through the last fringe of the forest.

"So now we're in the pink, eh?" With a last convulsive snort, Kabumpo stuffed the handkerchief into a lower pocket and trumpeted three times for Thun to halt. "Are those flowers, d'ye 'spose? May I see one of them, my dear?"

Catching up with the little Princess who was already on the edge of the field, Kabumpo took the long spray she had picked and passed it back to Randy.

"My gooseness, it's a feather! The largest and finest I've ever seen," Randy said in surprise. "Hey, I always thought feathers grew on birds, yet here's a whole field of feathers, Kabumpo—imagine that! And taller than I am, too."

"Well, there's no harm in feathers," observed Kabumpo jocularly. "Pick a plume for your bonnet, my child. The girls in our countries adorn themselves with these pretty fripperies. I've even worn them myself at court functions," he admitted self-consciously. "But do you think you can hold the colt's head up as we go through? Burnt feathers smell rather awful, and we don't wish to anger the owner or spoil his crop."

A bit confused by the word "owner" and "crop," Planetty nevertheless caught the idea and explained it so cleverly to Thun, the Thunder Colt started through the field, holding his head high and handsome so that the flames spurted upward and not down.

"It was rather like ploughing through a wheat field," decided Randy as Kabumpo, treading lightly as he could, stepped after Thun. It was, though, more like a sea of waving plumes, endlessly bending, nodding and rippling in the wind. Planetty gathered armfuls of these bright and newest treasures, liking them almost as much as the flowers in the forest. Thun, for his part, found the whole experience irksome in the extreme.

"These pink feathers give me the big pain in the neck," he puffed up indignantly as he trotted along with his head in the air. Planetty, reading his message with a little smile, was astonished to hear a series of roars and explosions behind her. Surely Thun's remarks were not as funny as all that! Turning round, she was shocked to see Kabumpo swaying and stumbling in his tracks, coughing and spluttering, and torn by such gigantic guffaws he had already shaken Randy from his back. The young King himself rolled and twisted on the ground, fairly gasping for breath.

"It's the feathers!" he gasped weakly, as Planetty, leaping off the Thunder Colt, ran back to investigate. "They're tickling us to death. Get away quickly, Netty, dear, before they get you—Oh, ha, ha, HAH! Oh, ho, ho! Quick! Before it is too late. Oh, hi, hi, hi! I shall die laughing!" To the startled little Princess he appeared to be dying already.

"No, no! Please not!" she cried, dropping her armful of feathers.

159

With surprising strength she jerked Randy upright and, in spite of his continued roars and wild writhing, managed to fling him across Thun's back. Now Kabumpo was down, kicking and rolling hysterically. It seemed to Planetty that the feathers were wickedly alive and tickling them on purpose. They tossed, swayed and brushed against her and Thun, too, but having no effect on the metalic skin of the Nuthers, curled away in distaste.

"Stop! Stop! I hate you!" screamed Planetty, stamping on the bunch she had picked a moment before, then struggling in vain to pull Kabumpo up by his trunk. "Thun! Thun! What shall we do?"

Racing back to the Thunder Colt, Planetty tapped out all that was happening to their best and only friends, holding the convulsed and still laughing Randy in place with one hand as she did so. Thun, from anxious glances over his shoulder, had guessed more than half the difficulty.

"Search in the Kabumpty's pocket for something to tie round him so I may pull him out of the feathers," flashed the Thunder Colt, swinging in a circle to prance and stamp on the plumes still curling down to tickle the helpless boy on his back.

Feeling in Kabumpo's pockets as he tossed and

lashed about was hard enough, but Planetty, who was quick and clever, soon found a long, stout, heavily linked gold chain Kabumpo twisted round and round his neck on important occasions. Slipping the chain through his belt, the little Princess clasped the other ends round the Thunder Colt's chest, making a strong and splendid harness. Then, mounting quickly and holding desperately to Randy, Planetty gave the signal for Thun to start. And away through the deadly field charged the night black steed, burning feathers left and right with his flashing breath and dragging Kabumpo along as easily as if he had been a sack of potatoes instead of a two-ton elephant. The feathers bending beneath made the going soft so that the Elegant Elephant did not suffer so much as a scratch, and Thun galloped so swiftly that in less than ten minutes they had reached the other side of the beautiful but treacherous field. Going half a mile beyond, Thun came to an anxious halt, the golden chain falling slack around his ankles, while Planetty jumped down to see how Kabumpo was doing now.

The Elegant Elephant had stopped laughing, but his eyes still rolled and his muscles still twitched and rippled from the terrible tickling he had endured. Randy, exhausted and weak, hung like a dummy

161

stuffed with straw over the Thunder Colt's back.

"Oh, we were too late, too long!" mourned Planetty, wringing her hands and running distractedly between the Elegant Elephant and the insensible King. "Oh, my netness, they will become stiff and still as Nuthers deprived of their springs," she tapped out dolefully to Thun.

"Do not be too sure." The Thunder Colt puffed out

his message slowly. "See, already the big Kabumpty is trying to rise."

And such, indeed, was the case. Astonished and mortified to find himself stretched on the ground in broad daylight and still too confused to realize what had happened, the Elegant Elephant lurched to his feet and stood blinking uncertainly around. Then, his eyes suddenly coming into proper focus, he caught sight of Randy lying limply across the Thunder Colt.

"What in Oz? What in Ix? What in Ev is the matter here?" he panted, wobbling dizzily over to Thun.

"Feathers!" sighed Planetty, clasping both arms round Kabumpo's trunk and beginning to pat and smooth its wrinkled surface. "The feathers tickled you and you fell down, my poor Bumpo. Randy too was almost laughed to the death. What does death mean?" Planetty looked up anxiously into his eyes.

"Great Grump! So that was it! Great Gillikens! I remember now, we were both nearly tickled to death and it was awful, AWFUL! Not that Ozians ever do die," he explained hastily, "but, after all, we are not in Oz and anything might have happened. And what I'd like to know is how in Ev we ever got out of those feathers."

"Thun pulled you out," Planetty told him proudly. "And look, LOOK, Bumpo dear, Randy is going to waken, too."

"Randy! Randy, do you hear that?" Kabumpo lifted the young King down and shook him gently backward and forward. "This colt of Planetty's, this Thunder Colt, all by himself, mind you, pulled us out of that infernal feather field! You and me, but mostly me. Now tell me how did he manage to pull an elephant all that way?"

Randy, only half comprehending what Kabumpo was saying, said nothing, but Thun, guessing Kabumpo's question, threw back his head and puffed quickly:

"We Nuthers are strong as iron, Master. Strong

for ourselves, strong for our friends. Thun, the Thunder Colt, will always be strong for Kabumpty!"

"Strong! Strong? Why, you're marvelous," gasped the Elegant Elephant.

Placing Randy on the ground, he fished jewels from his pocket with a reckless trunk till he found a band of pearls to fit Thun. Then carelessly risking the sparks from the Thunder Colt's nostrils, he fastened the pearls in place.

"Tell him, tell him THANKS!" he blurted out breathlessly. "Tell him from now on we are friends and equals, friends and warriors, together!"

With a pleased nod Planetty translated for Thun, and the delighted colt, tossing his flying mane, raced round and round his three comrades, filling the air with high-flown and flaming sentences.

"Friends and warriors!" he heralded, rearing joyously. "Friends and warriors!"

By this time Randy had recovered his breath and his memory and felt not only able but impatient to continue the journey. The field of feathers could still be seen waving pink and provokingly in the distance, but without one backward glance the four travelers set their faces to the north. A few of Chillywalla's boxes had been crushed while Kabumpo rolled in the feathers, and he and Randy still felt weak and worn from their dreadful experience, but these were small matters when they considered the dreadful fate they had escaped through the quick action of Planetty and Thun.

"I always thought of Ix as a pleasant country," sighed Randy as Kabumpo moved slowly along a shady by-path.

"I don't believe this is Ix," stated the Elegant Elephant bluntly. "The air's different, smells salty, and this sandy road looks as if we might be near the sea. I think myself that we've come north by east through Ix into Ev and will reach the Nonestic Ocean by evening." Kabumpo paused to peer up at a rough board nailed to a pine.

"So! You got through the feathers, did you?" sneered the notice in threatening red letters. "Then so much the worse for you! Beware! Watch out! Gludwig the Glubrious has his eye on you."

"Glubrious!" sniffed Kabumpo, elevating his trunk scornfully as Randy read and re-read the impertinent message. "I don't recall anyone named Gludwig, do you?"

"Sounds rather awful, doesn't it?" whispered Randy, sliding to the ground to examine the billboard from all sides. "Say, look here, Kabumpo, there's something on the back. It's been scratched out with red chalk, but I can still read it."

"Then read it," advised Kabumpo briefly.

"This is the Land of Ev! Everybody welcome! Take this road to the Castle of the Red Jinn."

"Oh, that means we're almost there!" exulted the young King, but his joy evaporated quickly as he re-read the other side of the board.

"Looks as if someone had switched signs on Jinnicky," he muttered, pushing back his crown with a little whistle. "Do you think anything has happened to him?"

"Probably some mischievous country boy trying

out his chalk," answered the Elegant Elephant, not believing one of his own words. "Straight on, my dear," he called cheerfully to Planetty, who had pulled in the colt and was looking questioningly back at them. "At last we are in the Land of Ev, and just ahead lies the castle of our wizard."

"Oh, Bumpo, how nite!" Planetty hugged herself from pure joy. "I've never seen a castle, I've never seen a wizard!"

167

"But, Kabumpo—" worried Randy as the little Princess of Anuther Planet galloped gaily ahead of them. "Suppose this Gludwig really has his eye on us? Suppose he rushes out before we can reach Jinnicky's castle?"

"Well, that will not be very 'nite,' will it?" The Elegant Elephant spoke ruefully. "But what can we do? Are we going to stop for a mere sign?"

"No!" declared Randy, feeling about for his sword. "Of course not. But I'll wager a Willikin he was the fellow who planted those feathers."

"Very likely," agreed Kabumpo, pushing grimly along through the sand.

CHAPTER 12

Arrival at the Castle of the Red Jinn

THE further they traveled into Ev, the more interesting the country became to Planetty and Thun. Now wild orange and lemon trees added their spicy tang to the salty air; waving palms edged the sandy roadway, and after traversing a grove of lordly cocoanut trees the four suddenly found themselves facing the great, green, rolling Nonestic.

"A spring!" caroled Planetty, galloping Thun down to the water's edge. "Oh, never have I seen so netiful a spring!"

"Not a spring, Princess, an ocean," corrected Ka-

bumpo, ambling good naturedly after Thun. "This is a salt salt sea, full of ships, sailors, shells, crabs, islands, fish and fishermen."

"And will I see all of them?" Slipping from Thun's back Planetty waded out a little way, hopping gleefully over the edges of the smaller waves.

"Some time," promised Randy, dismounting hastily to keep her from venturing too far. "Look over your shoulder, Netty," he urged, drawing her back toward shore, "and then tell me what you think!"

Explaining this gay, wide and wonderful world to the little Princess of Anuther Planet, Randy found more fun than anything he had ever done or imagined. Tense with expectation, he and Kabumpo watched as Planetty gazed off to the right.

"Why—'tis a high, high hill of red that glitters! Or what? What is it?" Planetty whirled Thun round so he could see, too.

"It's a castle, m'lass." Kabumpo swaggered down the beach, as if he alone were responsible for all its splendor and magnificence. "There you see the imperial palace of the Wizard of Ev, built from turret to cellar of finest red glass studded with rubies, and there, this night, we will be suitably entertained by Jinnicky himself."

"The inside's even better than the outside," Randy whispered in Planetty's ear, as she tapped out this astonishing news to the Thunder Colt. "Come on, come on, it's not more than a mile, and we can go straight along the edge of the sea shore. Say, weren't we lucky not to run into Gludwig?" Pulling himself up on Kabumpo's back, Randy spoke the words softly. "It would have been too bad to have the first person outside of ourselves that Planetty met turn out a villain. I believe that sign WAS a joke."

"Well, everything seems all right so far," admitted

the Elegant Elephant guardedly. "But keep your eyes open, my boy—keep your eyes open. Is that a welcome committee marching along the beach, or is it an army?"

"They're still too far away to tell," answered Randy. "Looks to me like all Jinnicky's blacks; I can see their baggy red trousers and turbans."

"Yes, but what's that gleaming in the sunlight?"

demanded Kabumpo, curling up his trunk uneasily.

"Only their scimiters," Randy said, standing up to have a better view. "Each man is carrying a scimiter over his shoulder, but that's perfectly all right, they're probably parading for our benefit."

"Mm-mm! Sometimes things are not what they scim-iter!" sniffed Kabumpo, snapping his eyes suspiciously. But Randy, paying no attention to the Elegant Elephant's remark, was feeling round in the net bags for Chillywalla's band box, and next moment the lively strains of a military march filled the air.

Swinging along in time to the music, Kabumpo peered sharply at the oncoming host for signs of Alibabble, or Ginger, the slave of the bell, or some of Jinicky's other old and trusted counselors. But in all that great throng there was no one familiar face, and because he was beginning to feel more than a bit worried, Kabumpo lifted his feet higher and higher. "Everything looks black, very black," he muttered dubiously.

"Why not?" cried Randy, waving his arms like a bandmaster. "They're all as black as the ace of spades. Mind you, Planetty, it takes all these black men to take care of Jinnicky and his castle."

"And will they take care of us?" Planetty eyed the marchers with positive amazement and alarm. "So many," she murmured in a hushed voice, "so black. I thought everyone down here would be like you and Bumpo."

"My, no," Randy told her complacently. "Everyone is liable to be different. I believe I'll toss out some of Chillywalla's boxes. Visitors should come bearing presents, you know!"

Hastily Randy began pulling out boxes of candy, boxes of cigarettes, beads, cigars and whole suits of clothing to dazzle Jinnicky's subjects. But when the leader of the procession came within ten feet of the travelers he threw back his head and emitted such a blood-curdling howl, Randy's hair rose on his head, and as the rest of the blacks, brandishing scimiters and yelling threats and imprecations, came leaping toward them, the desperate young King began hurling down boxes as if they were bombs. He caught the Headman on the chin with the bandbox, but while it stopped the music it did not stop the gigantic Evian from slashing at Thun. As his scimiter fell, Kabumpo gave a trumpet that felled the whole front rank of the enemy, and snatching up the villain in his trunk, he hurled him back among his men.

174

Chapter Twelve

"Is this—is this taking care of us?" shuddered Planetty, clasping her arms round the neck of the plunging Thunder Colt.

"No, no! My goodness, NO! Is Thun hurt? Quick, Kabumpo!" screamed Randy as a second scimiter slashed down on Thun's flank. Then he managed to breathe again, for the razor-sharp weapon glanced harmlessly off the metal coat of Planetty's coal black charger. The wielder of the scimiter, however, did not escape so easily, for a hot blast from Thun's nostrils sent him reeling backward.

"That's it! Give it to them! Give it to them!" shouted Randy, forgetting in his excitement that Thun could not hear, and he himself hurled Chilly-walla's boxes hard and viciously and one after the other. As for Kabumpo, every time he raised his trunk there was a black man in it, and as fast as they came he slung them over his shoulder.

But it was Planetty who really turned the tide of battle. While Randy, who had exhausted his supply of boxes, was digging desperately in Kabumpo's pockets for some more missiles, he heard a perfect chorus of terrified screeches. Popping up with an umbrella and an alarm clock, he saw the Princess of Anuther Planet standing erect on the galloping colt's

The Silver Princess in Oz

back, calmly and precisely casting her staff at the foe. Each time the staff struck, the victim, in whatever attitude he happened to be, was frozen into a motionless metal figure. After each stroke the staff returned to Planetty's hand.

"Yah, yah, mah—MASTER!" wailed the frantic

blacks who were still able to move, and tumbling over one another in their effort to escape, they fled wildly back to the Red Castle, leaving behind sixty of their vanquished brethren.

"You—you—YOU'LL be sorry for this!" shouted the Headman, tearing off his turban and waving it as he ran.

"So will you!" bellowed Kabumpo fiercely. "Just wait till Jinnicky hears about this! How dare you treat his visitors in this violent wicked fashion?"

"Jinnicky! Jinnicky!" jeered the Headman as Planetty aimed her staff threateningly at his back. "Jinnicky is at the bottom of the sea!"

"Mm—Mnnn! Mnmph! I knew it, I knew it!" groaned the Elegant Elephant as the Headman reached the palace and scittered wildly up the glass steps. "I knew something was wrong the moment I saw those scimiters."

"Jinnicky gone! Jinnicky at the bottom of the sea? Why, I just can't believe it!" Randy, glancing over his shoulder at the tumbling Nonestic, looked almost ready to cry. Then putting back his shoulders, he declared fiercely, "Well, I'M not going off and leave this old pirate in Jinnicky's castle, are you? It must be Gludwig's doing—all this! Let's go inside and throw him out of there! We have lots of help now. Thun's a regular flame thrower and Planetty's worth a whole army, and best of all nothing can hurt them. Why didn't you tell me you had a magic staff?" Randy looked admiringly down at the resolute little Princess at his side. "Why, with that staff we can conquer anybody."

"Is that what you call the magic?" Planetty regarded her staff with new interest.

"It certainly is!" panted Kabumpo, fanning himself with a handy palm leaf. "And we're mighty

179

sorry to have gotten you into all this danger and trouble, my dear. Looks as if we had a war on our hands instead of a pleasant vacation."

"Oh, that! It is nothing, nothing!" Planetty shrugged her shoulders eloquently. "On our planet we too have the bad beasts and Nuthers, and when they try to hit or bite us, we just subdue them with our voral staffs."

"Mmmn—mn! So I see." Kabumpo, still fanning himself, looked thoughtfully at Gludwig's petrified warriors. "There must be a goodly bit of statuary on your planet, m'lass?"

"Very many," answered Planetty soberly, polishing her staff on the end of her cape. With a slight shudder the Elegant Elephant turned from the fallen slaves, resolving then and there never to offend this pretty but powerful little metal maiden.

"Well, have the scoundrels dispersed and gone for good?" inquired Thun, sending up his question in a cloud of black smoke. Restively pawing the ground, the Thunder Colt looked from one to the other waiting for someone to enlighten him.

"Tell him they've gone, but for nobody's good," wheezed Kabumpo, who was still out of breath from the violence of the combat. "Tell him Gludwig the

180

Chapter Twelve

Glubrious has destroyed the Wizard of Ev and that we are now going into the castle to continue the battle."

"But where shall we start?" sighed Randy, staring despondently up at the gay red palace where he and Kabumpo had been so royally entertained on their last visit.

"We'll start at the bottom of these steps," announced Kabumpo grimly, "and mount on up to the top. Then we'll burst into the presence of this wretched wart and fling him out of the window."

"But that won't help Jinnicky if he's at the bottom of the sea," mourned Randy, trying to smile at Planetty, who was busily tapping off instructions to Thun.

"Hah! but don't forget, Jinnicky's a wizard," sniffed Kabumpo, pulling in his belt a few inches, "and nobody can keep a good wizard down. Besides," Kabumpo dragged his robe a bit to the left and straightened his headpiece, "once inside that castle, we can use some of the Red Jinn's own magic to help him."

"Magic? Why, of course, I'd forgotten about that." Randy's face cleared and brightened and seeing Planetty and Thun so eager and unafraid beside him, he girded on his sword and standing upright on Kabumpo's back, gave the signal to start. As they trod up the hundred red glass steps they could hear windows and doors slamming, the patter of running feet and the tinkle of the hundred glass chimes in the tower. But step by step, and without a pause, Thun and Kabumpo mounted to the top.

"Beware! Beware, Gludwig the Glubrious! Here march Kabumpty and Thun, Slandy and Planetty,

Princess of Anuther Planet. Friends, equals and warriors!"

The Thunder Colt's flaming message, floating like a battle emblem in the air, alarmed the wicked occupant of Jinnicky's castle even more than the invaders themselves. But still confident of his power to vanquish all comers, he waited in evil anticipation for the moment when they would force their way into his presence. Did they imagine because they had frightened a company of foolish slaves they could frighten him?

"Ha, ha!" Crouched on the Red Jinn's throne and laughing mirthlessly, Gludwig rubbed his long hands up and down his skinny knees.

CHAPTER 13

Gludwig the Glubrious

PSS-SST! Wait! Hold on a minute!" As they
reached the huge double doors of the red castle,
Randy tugged violently at Kabumpo's left ear, for
the Elegant Elephant, all humped together, was pre-
paring to bump through. "Let Thun break down the
door," directed the young King firmly. "Thun is of
metal and the glass will not cut him; then, as soon
as there is an opening we can follow. Will you tell
him, Planetty?" Randy looked fondly down at the
earnest little Princess. "And as soon as we are inside," he went on hurriedly, "fling your staff at the
first person I point out to you."

184

Chapter Thirteen

"That I will," promised Planetty with a brief nod, and giving Thun his orders, she galloped the Thunder Colt straight at the glass doors. With a crash like the fall of a hundred trays of dishes, the glass doors shivered to bits. Rushing through the flying splinters, Kabumpo and Thun raced together into the palace.

How well Randy remembered this cozy throne room, its transparent, red glass pillars and floors, its gay, red lacquered furniture, its tinkling curtains of strung rubies, and the long line of enormous red vases leading up to the throne. But instead of the jolly little Jinn, encased in his own shining jar, a long, lank black man in a red wig lounged on the seat of state. He was smoking a tenuous red pipe, and, as Kabumpo and Thun came to an abrupt halt before him, he blinked wickedly out from under his bushy red lashes. Besides the red-wigged imposter Randy noted with some relief, there was not another soul in sight.

"Well," demanded Gludwig, insolently, "what do you hope to accomplish by this unwarranted intrusion?" Taking his pipe out of his mouth, he blew a cloud of villainous black smoke into the faces of his visitors. So thick and sulphurous were the fumes,

185

Randy and Kabumpo were rendered speechless. While they choked and spluttered, Planetty, who did not seem aware of the smoke at all, gazed in wide-eyed delight around her. So THIS was a castle!

"How nite, how netiful!" Lost in wonder and admiration, the little Princess forgot all about the stern purpose of their visit.

"Off that throne! Off that throne, you wart!" rasped Kabumpo, clearing his throat with an ear-splitting trumpet. "What have you done with Jinnicky? You're no more a wizard than I am! You're as false and crooked as your wig! Down with him! Down with him, Randy! Let him repent of his wickedness in uttermost disgrace and debasement!"

"So my downfall is the little plan?" Speaking calmly, but trembling with fury at Kabumpo's taunting speech, Gludwig rose. At the same instant Randy, recovering his breath, called desperately.

"Now, Planetty, your staff! Throw it straight at him. Oh, quickly!"

Thun's hot breath was already singeing Gludwig's ankles, and, leaping over the throne, he crouched down like a great black panther behind it.

"Ha, ha!" he shouted again. "My downfall and

189

debasement is it? Well, try a bit of downfalling and debasement yourselves."

Just as Planetty, taking careful aim, hurled her gleaming staff, Gludwig pulled a tremendous lever in the wall beside him. Instantly the floor on the other side of the throne dropped down, slanting Ka-

bumpo, Thun and both riders into the dark, damp and long-unused cellar of the castle.

"A trap door," raged the Elegant Elephant, coming down like a carload of bricks.

"A trap floor, you mean," gasped Randy, picking himself up with a painful grimace, for the jolt had sent him flying off the elephant. Thun had retained his balance, and neither he nor Planetty seemed to mind the force of their landing. As they gazed angrily upward, the floor of the throne room swung noiselessly back into place, leaving the four prisoners to contemplate the heavy glass beams and panels of its under side.

"So that was the downfall, and this is debasement," grunted Kabumpo, sitting down furiously on an over-turned wash-tub. "Great Grump, I've never been so

humiliated in my life. Don't cry, Planetty," he begged gruffly, "we'll have you out of here in a pig's whistle."

"It's not that, Bumpo, dear." Planetty buried her face in Thun's cloudy mane and sobbed bitterly. "It's my staff! It did not return after I flung it at the red-wigged one, and without it I have nothing, NOTH-ING!"

"Good Gollopers!" Randy clapped his hand to his forehead as he realized the awful significance of Planetty's disclosure. "The floor tilted too quickly for it to return, and OH, KABUMPO!" he wailed, almost forgetting he was a King and Warrior. "If Gludwig has that staff, what can we do? He can come down here and petrify us any time he wants."

"We'll hide!" gulped Kabumpo, bounding off the wash-tub. With furious concentration his small eyes roved round and round their gloomy prison.

"But you're so big," declared Randy, running over to comfort Planetty.

"I'll hide anyway!" said Kabumpo, who had no intention of spending the rest of his life as an iron elephant, nor of adorning the palace of Gludwig the Glubrious as the mere image of himself.

CHAPTER 14

The Slave of the Magic Dinner Bell

HOW thankful Randy and Kabumpo were now for the Thunder Colt's fiery breath. Otherwise they would have been in almost complete darkness, as scarcely any light at all trickled down through the dark red glass of the cellar windows. And there was small danger of his setting Jinnicky's castle on fire, for the basement, like the rest of the palace, was constructed of thick plates of solid glass. But here below, the glass was not bright and sparkling as it was above stairs. Cobwebs clung to the glass beams, dust powdered the floors, and round the walls in boxes and barrels stood the old or worn out magic appliances of the Red Jinn. There was no furnace in the

193

cellar, for the castle was warmed in winter by a magic process of Jinnicky's own invention; and there were no doors, not even a closet or cupboard where any of them could hide. With Thun stepping ahead to act as a torch, the others marched anxiously round the great gloomy vault-like apartment.

"No place to hide, no provisions, nothing to eat or drink. NOTHING!" exclaimed the Elegant Elephant, sinking down on the wash-tub. "That is, nothing to do but wait for destruction," he concluded bitterly.

"Well, we're not destroyed yet!" declared Randy, sticking out his chin. "Everything seems quiet above. Maybe Gludwig is not going to use Planetty's staff till morning."

With a discouraged sniff Kabumpo began poking in the boxes behind him. Finding one full of excelsior, he started to stuff the choking material into his mouth with his trunk. Randy was sure the excelsior would disagree with him, but when Kabumpo was in such a mood, it was quite useless to argue with him; so, beckoning for Thun to light the way, he and Planetty set out on a second tour of investigation.

Randy paused dubiously before a collection of squat bottles and jugs. He was convinced they contained liquids or vapors powerful enough to help them, but the directions on the labels were all in some strange magician's code and Randy hesitated to open even one of the magic bottles. Experience had taught him that a wizard's wares were dangerous, and he himself had seen the Red Jinn subdue whole armies by releasing incense from a blue jug. So, selecting two pocket-size jars, to use only in case everything else failed, Randy moved on to the other side of the cellar. Here on top of a chest he discovered a small red hand-bag. Instead of the usual fastenings, two real hands formed the clasp, and when Randy opened the bag it quickly jerked out of his grasp and began springing all over the cellar on its hands, pouncing gleefully on papers and bottles and stuffing them into its side pockets. It did look so comical, Planetty burst into a peal of merriment. Even Randy could not keep back a grin. It was a relief to see the little Princess more like herself again, for since the loss of her voral staff she had been unnaturally quiet and sad.

"Wait, I'll catch it for you," offered Randy, dismissing for a moment all thought of the dreadful danger they were in. "It must be one of Jinnicky's inventions. Look, Kabumpo, a bag that really packs itself."

195

"Watch out it doesn't pinch you!" warned Kabumpo morosely. He had already begun to regret the excelsior and was rumbling with indigestion. "I was never one to hold with hand luggage, myself."

"Oh, yes you were!" crowed Randy, falling on the bag as if it had been a football and coming up tri-

umphantly with it clutched to his middle. "You use your trunk for a hand, Kabumpo, and doesn't that make it hand luggage? Hey, hey, hurray! Never thought I'd make a joke in this dismal place!"

"It's a pretty dismal joke, if you ask me." The Elegant Elephant heaved himself stiffly off the washtub. "Keep it away from me!" he warned crossly, as Randy, paying no attention to the thumps of the hand-bag, managed to get it shut again. As soon as

196

it was closed the bag subsided and seemed absolutely unalive. "Here!" puffed Randy, holding it out to Planetty. "This bag will pack itself, madam, and you can use it every time you go on a journey."

"Can I? How nite!" Planetty beamed at her young companion.

"Well, who's going on a journey?" inquired Kabumpo sarcastically, walking up and down to relieve his indigestion. "We'll probably spend the rest of our unnatural lives in this abominable basement. Say something, can't you?" he shouted, glaring at poor Thun. "I can hardly see where I'm going." As fast as Planetty translated this rude speech, the Thunder Colt sent up his answer.

"If I said all the words I am thinking," puffed Thun temperishly, "this room would be very red bright, Mister Kabumpty, very red bright indeed." The Thunder Colt's speech and his further remarks made Randy and Planetty laugh again.

"Let's see what else we can find," proposed the young King. In spite of Kabumpo's gloomy predictions, he was feeling more hopeful. "Maybe this time we'll turn up something we can really use."

"Oh, maybe yes, maybe yes!" trilled Planetty, slipping swiftly as quicksilver after Randy. Passing by some dusty apparatus and an old spinning wheel, they discovered a huge red drum behind a pile of old trunks. The sticks were stuck through a cord in the side and it was so heavy that the two between them could hardly carry it. But giggling and puffing they dragged it into the center of the cellar and dropped it down before Kabumpo.

"See what we have now!" Dusting off his clothes, Randy surveyed it proudly.

"Humph! A DRUM!" The Elegant Elephant moved his ears forward and then back. "Well, what grumpy use is a drum? Am I in a parade? Do you expect me to beat it?"

"Beat the drum?" Planetty looked surprised and shocked. "Is that for what a drum is for, Bumpo, dear?"

"Well, yes, in a way." A bit ashamed of himself, Kabumpo drew out one of the sticks. "It goes like this," he said, raising the drumstick high in his trunk.

"Oh no! Kabumpo, NO! Don't do that or you'll have Gludwig down here! It would make too much noise."

"What if it does?" Kabumpo shrugged his great shoulders. "We may as well perish now as tomorrow. I'm perishing of hunger anyway."

199

Before Randy could interfere, he brought the drumstick down with a thump that split the taut surface of the drum from edge to edge. The loud rip and BONG made the rafters ring, and scarcely had they recovered from that shock before a small black boy in an enormous turban sprang out of the drum itself and began sobbing and spluttering and hugging Kabumpo as if he never would let him go.

"Good Gillikens! It's Ginger!" panted Randy, as Planetty caught him anxiously by the sleeve. "It's the slave of the magic dinner bell. He can bring us dinners and whatever one wants when Jinnicky rings for him. Hi—who shut you up in that drum, boy?"

"That big old Red Wig," sniffed Ginger, drying his tears on Kabumpo's robe. "Oh, how can I ever thank you, Mister Elephant so Elegant! I remember you! I remember him!" The bell boy jerked his thumb delightedly at Randy. "And many times I thank you—fifty times eleven, I thank you. You see, if I am shut up in a drum, it is impossible for me to answer the Master's ring if he needs me. And he needs me now, I know it, I know it!"

"But how can he call you unless he has the dinner bell?" asked Randy, edging closer. "Did Jinnicky take the bell with him when—when—" To save himself, Randy could not finish the dismal sentence.

"When Gludwig pushed him into the sea, you mean?" Ginger's brown face puckered up again, but, controlling his sobs with a great effort, he sat down on the edge of the drum and told them the whole story of Jinnicky's mischance and misfortunes.

"The Master, as you know," explained Ginger, his eyes rolling sideways as he caught sight of Planetty and Thun, whose like he had never seen in his entire magic existence, "the Master is always kind and jolly and unsuspecting. This Gludwig was the manager of our ruby mines and one of Jinnicky's most trusted officers. But all the time, this viper, this snake, this villainous black snake—" Ginger clenched his fists and kicked his heels angrily against the drum— "was planning to steal our Red Jinn's throne and magic, in addition to his own splendid mansion and fortune. One evening, seven moons ago, having trained his miners into an army of rebellion, Gludwig marched upon our castle and drove everybody out."

"Everybody?" The Elegant Elephant, picking Ginger up in his trunk, looked earnestly into his face.

"Every EV body!" repeated the little bell boy, wagging his turban sorrowfully. "Alibabble, the Grand Advizier, all the members of the court and household were sent to the mines under the cruel rule of Glubdo, Gludwig's brother, and they are

there now, working without rest, hope or reward. He marched the Master to the head of the highest cliff and pushed him violently into the sea with his OWN hands!"

Ginger began to tremble with grief and anger at the memory of it all. He ordered the bandsmen to seal me up in this drum, knowing a drum is the only place from which I cannot escape, and hoping I would shrivel up and perish. But I—" asserted the

202

little black triumphantly—"I am the best part of Jinnicky's magic, so he couldn't destroy me." A quick grin overspread Ginger's face. "And he could not destroy my Master either. Of that I am sure, and now that the elephant so elegant has let me out —NOW—"

"Now what?" breathed Randy, almost afraid Ginger was not going to tell him. "You see, Ginger, we came to visit the Red Jinn and were immediately captured and dumped down here ourselves. So how can we get out? And what can we do?"

"I will think of something," promised the bell boy. Wriggling out of Kabumpo's trunk, he scurried across the cellar and disappeared beneath an overturned wheelbarrow.

"So! He will think of something," sniffed Kabumpo, trying not to make it sound too sarcastic. "Well, of course, that settles it. And while he is thinking, I intend to take a nap. I'm completely worn out with all these vile plots and villainies."

"I too will ret," decided Planetty, reaching over to pat the Thunder Colt. The strange excitements of the day had wearied the little Princess, and this last story of Ginger's had still further puzzled and distressed her.

"I never thought when I brought you here you'd have to sleep in a place like this," groaned Randy, glancing ruefully round the dingy basement.

"Oh, it's not so bad," smiled the little Princess. Slipping off her cape, she swung it casually between two grimy pillars, and with the hand-bag tucked under her arm, climbed contentedly into her silver bed. "Good net, Randy and Bumpo, dear!" she called softly. "I believe I shall ret for a long, long time."

"Now what does she mean by that?" worried the young King, as the Princess blew them each a wistful kiss. "Something's wrong, Kabumpo, I feel it! And look there at Thun! Why is he acting so strangely? Almost as if he could not see."

"Look at him! Look at him!" wailed the Elegant Elephant. "Where is he? How can I? It's dark as thunder in here now! Great Grump, Randy, I can't see you, him or anything at all."

Stumbling and tripping, he somehow crossed the cellar to the spot where he remembered Thun had been. Then, as his trunk struck against hard cold metal, he recoiled in horror.

"He's OUT!" moaned the Elegant Elephant hoarsely. "He's not even breathing. Why, he's cold and stiff as a stone. Oh, Good Grump, the colt saved

204

my life and now what can I do for him? What'll we do, Randy? I say, what'll we DO?"

Randy had no answer at all, for, moved by a dreadful foreboding, he leaned down to touch the face of the little Princess of Anuther Planet, only to find it still and cold. No sparkling light radiated from Planetty now as, quiet and motionless as a statue, she lay wrapped in her silver nets.

"Ginger, where are you? Ginger, come help us!" Randy screamed desperately. Scrambling out from under the barrow, the startled bell boy reached Randy's side in a split second, for Ginger could see as well in the dark as in the daytime.

"Did—Gludwig—do—this?" he panted, his eyes rolling wildly from Planetty to the frozen Thunder Colt.

"No, no, they are far from their own country and need the powerful Vanadium springs," groaned Kabumpo, putting out his trunk to touch the little Princess. "They cannot exist down here. And with Jinnicky gone, who's to help them?" His tears fell thick and fast on Planetty's silver tresses.

"Then why do we stay here?" shuddered Ginger, tugging at Randy's cloak and Kabumpo's robe. "Why do we stay?"

As if to answer Ginger's mournful cry, there was a long whistling rustle in the air, and next moment Randy, Ginger, Kabumpo and the Princess of An-

uther Planet were wafted like feathers through the night, passing easily as mist through the narrow glass windows, up over the castle itself and out over the silvery moonlit sea.

CHAPTER 15

Nonagon Island

THE same afternoon the four travelers arrived at the Red Jinn's castle, a lonely fisherman in an odd nine-sided dory pulled out from the Nonagon Isle. This strange small nine-sided island lies about ninety leagues from the mainland of Ev. Flat, barren and rocky, it affords but a meager living to the nine fishermen who are its sole inhabitants. Each keeps strictly to his own side of the island, subsisting frugally on fish and the few poor vegetables he can grow in his rocky little garden. Hard and unfriendly as their island itself, the nine Nonagons go their own ways, exchanging brief nods on the rare occasions when they meet one another.

The habit of silence had so grown upon Bloff, the fisherman in the nine-sided dory, he did not even talk to the cat who shared his rough dwelling and accompanied him on all of his fishing trips. And so accustomed was poor Nina to her gruff and taciturn master that she expected nothing from him but an occasional kick or fish head. Never sure which would be forthcoming, she kept her green eyes watchfully upon him at all times. This afternoon she was certain it would be a fish head, and as Bloff reached the spot where he had set his nets her tail began to wave gently in pleasant anticipation.

Bloff himself seemed a little less grim, for the net seemed quite heavy, and sure he had made a good haul, he began pulling on the lines. But when his net came wet and dripping over the side of the boat, he gave a grunt of anger. In it were only three small fish and an immense red jug. His first impulse was to toss the jug back into the sea, but reflecting grumpily that he could use it to salt down fish for the winter, he rolled it into the bottom of the boat and, kicking the disappointed cat out of the way, rowed rapidly back to the island.

Chapter Fifteen

Stamping into his nine-sided shack with the net over his shoulder, Bloff banged the jug down on the hearth, cleaned and cut up the fish and popped them into a pot hung on a crane over the fire. Then, lighting his one poor lamp, he sat sullenly down to wait for his supper. The fish heads he flung cruelly into the hot ashes, and whenever he dozed for a

moment Nina tried to pull one out with her paw, for she knew full well she could get nothing else to eat.

For perhaps an hour there was not a sound in the fisherman's hut except the crackling of the driftwood in the grate and the hoarse breathing of the fisherman himself. Then suddenly Nina, who had almost succeeded in dragging her supper from the flames, gave a frightened backward leap.

"Oh, my, mercy me! Mercy, me!" came a muffled but merry voice. "Where—but where am I now?"

As Nina and her master turned startled eyes toward the red jug, for the voice was undoubtedly coming from the jug, the lid slowly lifted and a round jolly face peered out at them. What he saw was so discouraging, Jinnicky—for of course it was Jinnicky—dropped back out of sight. The magic fluid with which he had sealed himself in the jug before Gludwig hurled him into the sea had been melted by the warmth of the fisherman's fire, and the same warmth had restored the little Red Jinn to his usual vigor and liveliness. In a sort of protective stupor he had managed to survive the long months at the bottom of the ocean. A quick thinker at all times, Jinnicky rapidly regained his senses and realized at once what had happened. A fortunate tide had carried him into this fisherman's net and at last he was on dry land again; and NOW to find and face the villain who had usurped his throne and castle.

"But why—why—" groaned the little Jinn dolefully, "with all the fishermen in the Nonestic Ocean did I have to be pulled out by this long-jawed fellow?"

Chapter Fifteen

Venturing another look, and at the same time thrusting his arms and legs out of their proper apertures in the jug, he saw that Bloff had seized an oar and seemed about ready to whack it down on his head.

"Non, non, NON! My good fellow!" puffed Jinnicky, fixing his rescuer with his bright glassy eye. "Put up your oar. This is no battle, and I have much to say that will interest you, but first of all I want to thank you for pulling me out of the ocean. Heartily! Heartily! A suitable reward will be sent you as soon as I get back—er—get back my castle."

To this polite speech Bloff paid no attention whatsoever, but Nina, liking the pleasant voice of this curious visitor, began rubbing herself against his ankles. "I am the Red Jinn of Ev!" announced the little Wizard, keeping a wary eye on the oar. "At present banished from my castle by the treachery of a trusted officer. In fact," Jinnicky tapped himself smartly on the jug, "this villain actually took everything I had and tossed me into the sea."

"What's wrong with the sea?" inquired the fisherman hoarsely. Never having seen anyone in his whole life but the eight other Nonagon Islanders, Bloff did not really believe what he saw now. "I'm asleep and having a nightmare," he concluded, grasping the oar more determinedly still. And we can hardly blame him, for a fellow whose body is a huge red vase into which he can draw his arms, legs and head, at will, is pretty hard for anyone to believe. Realizing he was getting nowhere and that

his grim and dour rescuer cared nothing about his troubles, past or present, Jinnicky decided to try another line.

"Perhaps you could tell me the name of this place and your own name?" he murmured politely.

"I am Bloff, my cat is Nina, and this is the Nonagon Island," announced the fisherman, frowning at the little Wizard.

"Ah, a nine-sided island!" The Red Jinn stretched

his arms and hopped up and down to get the kinks out of his legs. "And I see you have a nine-sided cottage and a cat with nine lives."

Picking up poor skinny Nina, who was purring for the first time in her life, Jinnicky stroked her back thoughtfully as he counted the nine pieces of furniture in the rude hut, noted that it was nine o'clock and the ninth of May. "But is NINE my lucky number?" he pondered wearily. Could this churlish fisherman ever be persuaded to sail him back to the mainland? Looking at Bloff out of the side of his eye, he very much doubted it. Though Bloff had put down the oar, his manner was anything but cordial.

"Are there any other people on the island?" asked Jinnicky, more to keep up the conversation than because he really wanted to know.

At his question Bloff put back his head and in a long singsong voice drawled, "Bluff, Bliff, Bleef, Blaff, Bloof, Blaaf, Bleof and Bluof!"

"Oh, my! Mercy me!" At each name Jinnicky gave a little jump, and as Bloff came to the end of the list he seated himself gingerly on the edge of the bench and stared into the fire. What could he hope from such people? Then suddenly in the midst of his worries he became aware of the fish chowder bubbling cozily on the crane and realized at the same instant his enormous and devouring hunger. After all, you know he had not eaten for seven months.

"Ah!" he beamed, extending both arms toward his host, "DINNER!"

"MY dinner." The two words were spoken so

gruffly, Jinnicky's heart fell with a loud clunk into his boots. Why, this was unbelievable! He, Jinnicky, the one and only Wizard of Ev, to be flouted and insulted by a miserable fisherman. Well, at least he could leave the fellow's miserable hut and try his luck with the other Islanders. Reflecting sadly that a wizard without his magic is no better off than any other man, the Red Jinn slid off the bench and started for the door, trying to walk in a calm and dignified manner. But half-way there a sharp grunt brought him up short.

"Aho, no you don't," rasped Bloff, catching up with him in two strides. "Where do you think you're going? STOP! I need that jug to salt my fish. Here, give it to me."

"Why, you—you miserable mollusk—don't you dare touch me!" panted the Red Jinn, trying to beat off the fisherman with his puny hands. "This jug—is—an—important—part of me. Without my jug I cannot live at all."

"And do you think I care for that?" sneered Bloff. "You're just an old lobster in a pot to me. Here, give me that jug!"

Seizing Jinnicky by both arms, Bloff tried to shake him out of the jug. Nina, enraged at such barbarous treatment of the only one who had ever been kind to her, proved an unexpected ally. Flying at the fisherman, she began to scratch and claw his face and hands so successfully Bloff had to drop Jinnicky to grab the cat. The force of the drop sent the Red Jinn rolling over and over, dislodging a small silver bell from a hidden pocket in his sleeve. As the bell fell tinkling to the flagstones, Jinnicky gave a bounce of relief. His magic dinner bell, and up his sleeve all the time! How had he ever forgotten it? Oh, now—now—if Ginger had not been destroyed by Gludwig, and just answered the bell, everything would be dif-

ferent. And Ginger DID answer the bell, and everything WAS different! My, yes. So different, Bloff threw the cat at Jinnicky and simply raced for the door. No wonder, in his small nine-sided shack were now an elephant carrying a silvery Princess in his trunk, a black boy in a tall turban and a white boy in a sparkling crown. With one more terrified glance, Bloff took to his heels and never stopped running till he was waist high in the Nonestic Ocean.

CHAPTER 16
All Together at Last

KABUMPO! Kabumpo! Randy! Oh, my mercy me!" Rolling to his feet, Jinnicky tottered over to the hearth and, encountering Ginger half-way there, clasped his faithful Bell Boy to his shiny glass bosom. "As soon as that bell rang I knew everything was going to be better," he puffed. "And I rather expected Ginger, but YOU! Why, my dear old Gaboscis, fancy meeting YOU here!"

"But I don't fancy it at all," grunted Kabumpo, placing the sleeping Princess gently down on the fisherman's bench and glancing disgustedly round the mean little hut. "How in Ev did you ever happen to be in such a place, how did you get here and where in Oz are we, anyway?"

"Oh, Jinnicky, are you really all right?" Grasping the little Wizard by both arms, Randy examined him carefully from top to toe. "Kabumpo and I came to see you, and instead of you, there was Gludwig in your castle. He told us you were at the bottom of the sea, and after first trying to destroy us with his army, he flung us into the castle basement. There we found Ginger sealed up in a big drum and we let him out, and after awhile, in a way I cannot figure out at all, we find ourselves here. How did it happen?"

"Why, Ginger brought you, of course." Releasing the little black boy from his tight embrace, Jinnicky planted a huge kiss on his ebony forehead, and with a flashing grin the slave of the bell vanished into space. "Don't worry! He's always going, but he'll come back any time I ring the bell. You must all have been touching Ginger when the bell rang, so naturally when Ginger answered the bell he brought you right along."

"Nothing natural about it," fumed Kabumpo, drawing his trunk wearily across his forehead.

"But you haven't told us how YOU got here," said Randy, bending over Planetty to see that she had made the trip without coming to any harm.

"And what is that, pray?" demanded the little Jinn, eyeing the sleeping Princess with round astonished eyes. "Something you brought me for a present? A pretty little idol you've stolen from some

heathen temple? My, mercy me! What a beauty it is! I'll mount it on a ruby pedestal and worship it all the rest of my days!"

"Oh, no, Jinnicky, no!" Randy's voice broke and he could not utter another word, try as he would. In puzzled concern the Red Jinn turned to Kabumpo.

"She's not a present, but she's an idol all right—

219

Randy's idol—and he intends to spend the rest of his life worshiping her, if I read the signals aright," said Kabumpo dryly. "There you see the Princess of Anuther Planet, old boy, and up to an hour ago she was as live and bright and happy as any of us."

"But what happened to her? Oh, my, mercy me, another mystery!" Jinnicky clasped his hands in genuine distress.

"Well, you tell us what happened to you, and then we'll tell you what happened to her and us," offered Kabumpo. "That is, if we don't die of hunger first."

"Hunger?" Jinnicky swallowed four times in rapid succession. "Oh, my, mercy me and us! You do not even know the meaning of the word! I have not eaten a bite for seven months! But, har, har, har! That is all over now. With my magic dinner bell right at hand, why should anyone be hungry? Four dinners and at once," beamed the Red Jinn, ringing it smartly. "See, my dear, I've not even forgotten you." Jinnicky leaned down to stroke Nina, who had hidden behind the hearth brush when so many strangers came dropping into the hut. "This valiant Nonagon Puss fought bravely in my defense and has thereby earned herself a place in my heart and castle for all the rest of her nine natural lives."

"But first you must get back your castle," said
Kabumpo as Jinnicky began dancing up and down
the room, the miserable cat hugged tightly in his

arms. Even Randy had to smile at that. No one could be around the little Jinn and stay sorrowful, and worried as he was over Planetty and Thun, the young King could not help feeling that now they were together everything was going to turn out right. Some how and way Jinnicky would help them.

"Isn't this like old times?" he beamed, bustling around like a busy host as Ginger, with four enormous trays balanced on his head, flashed down, set an appetizing dinner before each of the company and melted away like smoke up the chimney. For Nina, he had brought nine saucers of cream and some minced chicken. For Kabumpo, a huge bowl of assorted nuts and another bowl of cut raw vegetables, each bowl capable of replenishing itself, so that there was enough for even an elephant. For Randy and Jinnicky there were the finest of roast duck dinners. So, forgetting their mean surroundings and Gludwig's wickedness, the three Royal Wayfarers fell to and ate with an abandon and gusto that would have astonished their own castleholds and footmen. Nina, lapping up her rich and plenteous viands, seemed to grow fat and content before their very eyes. And while they dined, Jinnicky explained how he had been tricked by Glud-

222

wig, pulled out of the sea by Bloff and then nearly shaken out of his jar by the surly fisherman, who at the same time had shaken out the bell and brought him assistance.

"Where is he? Wait till I get my trunk on him," raged Kabumpo, glancing sharply round the nine-sided shack. Jinnicky, on his part, when he discovered how Gludwig had treated his friends and visitors, was no less enraged and indignant.

"Used my very own patented trap floor on you, did he? Hah! wait—I'll fix him!" Beating his small hands angrily together, Jinnicky's eyes burned with a bright red hatred.

"Yes, we were floored, all right," admitted the Elegant Elephant, pushing away his two bowls, for at last he had had enough, and while Randy and the Red Jinn were finishing their suppers he told the whole story of their journey through Oz and Ev and Ix, of their meeting with Planetty and Thun and the sad fate that had overtaken these loyal comrades in the Red Castle when they could no longer avail themselves of their own Vanadium Springs.

"Vanadium?" murmured the Red Jinn, resting his head in his chubby hands. "I believe I could make a substitute for that. Why, in my laboratory—"

223

The Silver Princess in Oz

"Yes, but this isn't your laboratory," sighed Randy, "and how ever are we to get off this nine-sided island if all the fishermen are as hateful as Bloff?"

"Har! har! har! Now that is the least of our troubles." Jinnicky waved airily to the owner of the cottage whose glum face had just appeared in the

window. "Ginger shall carry us back, as easily as he carries the trays! First I shall ring the dinner bell, then when Ginger appears, I shall hang on to his coat; you, Randy, must hang on to me and Kabumpo, bless his big heart, shall hang on to you, being careful to hold the Princess of this Other Planet in his trunk. Oh, my, mercy me! I'd almost forgotten the cat."

224

Chapter Sixteen

Scooping up Nina, Jinnicky waited till the Elegant Elephant had lifted Planetty in his trunk, then, taking the silver bell from his sleeve, he gave it a cheerful tinkle.

"Ho, this!" puffed the little Jinn, blowing a kiss to the glowering fisherman—"this is the finest place to leave I've ever left in my whole life. Oh, my, mercy me! You and us! Here's Ginger! Hold on, everybody! We're OFF!"

And they were, sailing along as smoothly behind the little slave of the bell as if they weighed nothing at all, and leaving Bloff running in frantic circles round his hut—for he was now more convinced than ever that this was a nightmare or that, worse still, he had taken entire leave of his wits and senses.

CHAPTER 17
In the Red Jinn's Castle

WHILE Jinnicky and his friends had been having all these ups and downs and hair-raising experiences, Gludwig had passed an exceedingly pleasant and profitable evening. As his enemies had dropped into the cellar of the castle, the silver staff of Planetty missing him by a wide margin had fallen harmlessly at his feet. Gludwig's army had had much to say of this terrible weapon, and picking it up, he turned it gloatingly over and over in his hands. It is true that he had all of Jinnicky's treasures and possessions, but in his whole seven months

226

in the castle he had not discovered a way to use any of the Red Jinn's magic, nor been able to cast a single spell or transformation. This had taken half the zest out of his victory. But here, he had a simple and easily managed magic weapon—or had he?

Frowning suddenly, Gludwig wondered whether it only worked for the silver war maiden who had used it so disastrously against his men. Well, he would quickly find that out. Stepping to the door, he whistled for the huge hound that guarded the outer passageway. As it came bounding to his side he hurled the silver staff at its head. As the staff struck, the hound's progress was instantly arrested and instead of a live dog, he had a life-sized bronze with a look in the eyes that made even Gludwig turn away. But the staff did work! As it returned to his black hand, Gludwig hurried out of the throne room, rushing here and there about the castle to cast the staff again and again at his unsuspecting aids and servants.

"Are you mad?" hissed Glubdo, coming upon his brother in the act of petrifying a small boot boy. "If you continue in this reckless fashion—who will do the work or wait upon us?"

"Oh, I've only tried it on a dozen or so," said Gludwig, holding the staff jealously behind his back. "Mind you don't overstep your authority, brother, or I might be tempted to use it on you."

Chuckling wickedly at Glubdo's shocked expression, Gludwig mounted to his own quarters and hastily throwing off his clothes, curled up in Jinnicky's sumptuous ruby trimmed four poster. He was too weary to descend to the cellar and deal with

his enemies, and resolving to finish them off the first thing in the morning, the miserable imposter fell asleep, Planetty's magic staff clutched tightly in his hands.

While he slumbered, strange things were happening below stairs, for just as the clock in the tower tolled two Ginger noiselessly set his royal passengers down in the deserted throne room and vanished away with a flashing smile.

Snapping on a ruby lamp, the Red Jinn looked around him with a long sigh of content. Motioning for Kabumpo to place the sleeping Princess on his comfortable cushioned throne, he tiptoed about, touching one after another of his possessions.

"Where do you suppose he is?" whispered Randy, treading close behind him.

"I don't suppose, I know," Jinnicky whispered back. "Where would he be but in my own royal bed? Come along; we'll take him by surprise and the ears and throw him out of the window. Careful now, boys, step softly! Confound the black-hearted scoundrel! He's been using the silver staff."

Sorrowfully the little Jinn paused before the statue of his favorite dog.

"Never mind," comforted Randy. "When you find a way to restore Planetty she'll find a way to undo this mischief, and you know you still have Nina."

"Yes," said Jinnicky, placing the Nonagon cat tenderly on a red cushion. "Come on, then, we'll creep up on him. Nobody's around, nobody's on guard, this should be easy." Stepping softly up the

229

broad stair, Kabumpo as lightly as any of them, the three made their way to Jinnicky's vast bed room.

"Leave him to me," begged the Elegant Elephant in a fierce whisper. "I'll wring his neck with my own trunk."

"No, wait—I'll ring my dinner bell," puffed Jinnicky, "and have Ginger carry him to the other side of the Nonestic Ocean."

"Even that wouldn't be far enough," muttered Randy, tiptoeing over to the bed. "If we just knew where he had hidden Planetty's staff we could turn him into a big brass monkey, for that's just what he looks like."

"Ho! I do, do I?" The unexpected interruption made them all jump. Gludwig, wakened by Kabumpo's first whisper, had lain silently watching from beneath his long lashes. Now tossing back the silk covers, he sprang up, throwing the staff straight at Randy's heart.

"Now let's see what you'll turn to," he panted savagely.

Too startled to move or act, Kabumpo and Jinnicky watched in fascinated horror as the staff struck. And strike it did, but instead of petrifying Randy, the rod passed like a flash of lightning through the young King's body and returned to Gludwig's hand, leaving Randy live and lively as ever he was, lively enough in fact to leap forward, snatch the dangerous weapon and bring it down hard on his red-wigged head. With a thud that splintered Jinnicky's best bed, Gludwig fell back.

"Hah! What did I tell you?" exclaimed Randy,

and indeed the former holder of the castle in his petrified condition looked as much like a brass monkey as Randy had said he would.

"Oh, my, mercy me! Oh, my! Oh, me!" With trembling fingers the Red Jinn began to feel Randy all over. "With my own eyes I saw that staff go through you, lad, yet here you are—no mark—no statue. I declare I, I'm—" With tears running down his nose, Jinnicky embraced Randy over and over.

"Out of that bed with you!" screamed Kabumpo, "OUT!" And winding his trunk round the rigid Gludwig, he flung him violently out of the window. As the image fell with a resounding clunk into the vegetable garden below, the Elegant Elephant sank on his haunches and mopped his brow with one of the red silk bed sheets.

"Never—never do I hope to live through such a moment again," he groaned, blowing his trunk explosively. "I thought you were frozen and done for, my boy—done for!" Rocking to and fro, Kabumpo blinked the tears out of his eyes.

"I don't understand yet why I wasn't," admitted Randy, wriggling out of Jinnicky's grasp and touching the spot where the staff had struck him.

"Someone or something was protecting you," declared the little Jinn, nodding his head like a mandarin. "Do you carry any charms or talismans against evil, my boy?"

"Not a one." Turning out his pockets, Randy displayed a collection of knives, rubber bands, coins and the other odds and ends that a man usually

stores in his pockets. Among the strange assort-
ment were two small squat jars and on these Jinnicky pounced with a triumphant little crow.

"Why, Randy Spandy Jack a Dandy, you have
two bottles of my best weapon turning elixir! How
did you happen to have them?"

"Those?" Randy squinted down at the bottles in
positive mystification. "Oh, I must have picked them
up in the cellar—of course I did, I remember dis-
tinctly now."

"Oh, glory be! Glory me! Har, har, har! Am I a
good wizard or am I a good wizard? And to think
you should have happened on the very thing you'd
be needing." Jinnicky danced in exuberant circles.

"Sh—hush! Somebody's coming." Crowding all
his belongings back into his pocket, Randy turned in
alarm. Half the courtiers and servants were crowd-
ed into the doorway. And when they saw Jinnicky
and his friends instead of Gludwig in the Royal
Apartment they began to back away in chagrin and
embarrassment.

"Oh, it's all right," Jinnicky waved airily. "You
threw in your fortunes with the wrong man, that's
all! You'll find Gludwig below in the cabbages. But
I forgive you! I forgive you!" he added impulsively

as his former mine workers began to stammer apologies and excuses. "Go back to your beds now, but see that breakfast is on time and hot and appetizing."

With an impatient nod of his head, Jinnicky dis-

missed them and, looking very downcast and crestfallen, they hurried away.

It was a long time before the Red Jinn and his rescuers could bring themselves to retire. There was so much to talk of, to wonder over and to plan. But finally, even Randy acknowledged that he was sleepy, and confident that Jinnicky would find some way to help Planetty and Thun in the morning, he curled up on a small red sofa and fell into a peaceful slumber. As for Kabumpo, he stretched out on the floor and Jinnicky, not caring to occupy a bed so recently slept in by Gludwig, made himself comfortable on a bear rug beside the Elegant Elephant, enjoying the first real rest he had had in seven long months.

CHAPTER 18

The Red Jinn Restored

WORD of his return had quickly spread through the Red Jinn's vast dominions, and when Jinnicky and his guests descended next morning a whole loyal black legion were cheering from the courtyard and lined up along the shore. After Gludwig had seized the castle and enslaved the household, the rest of the natives had fled for their lives, refusing to stay or acknowledge the red-wigged imposter as their ruler. Now that Jinnicky was restored and safely at home again, their joy

Chapter Eighteen

knew no bounds. Appearing briefly on one of the castle balconies, the Red Jinn made one of his best and merriest speeches, telling of his experiences and assuring his faithful flock that Gludwig was gone and would trouble them no more. To prove his statement, he pointed to the fallen figure in the cabbage patch. Glubdo, fearing Jinnicky's anger, had already left for an unknown destination, and now there was nothing to be done but restore the Kingdom to its former cheerful status and prosperity.

While the Red Jinn, Kabumpo, Randy and Nina breakfasted happily on the terrace, a willing delegation marched off to the ruby mines to release Alibabble, the courtiers and servants from their long servitude. The miners who had taken their place in the castle and army were only too willing to return to the mines, for with Jinnicky back in power their hours were short, their wages high and each miner had his own cozy cottage and garden. The petrified miners who had served in the army that issued out to capture Randy and Kabumpo were stood along the highways to act as sign posts and also as warnings to all of the hard fate awaiting those who lent their ears to treachery and their arms to rebellion. Randy could hardly contain himself while all these necessary matters were attended to. The young monarch spent nearly all his time arranging and rearranging the cushions on Jinnicky's throne, where Planetty still lay in complete beauty and insensibility. Kabumpo was almost as bad, pacing anxiously between the throne and the terrace where Thun had been carried by fifty interested blacks.

"Even if I cannot bring them back to life and activity, they are a handsome addition to any castle," puffed Jinnicky, sinking down at last on one of his red lacquer sofas and fanning himself rapidly with his lid. "Oh, my mercy me! Don't look at me that way, my boy! Of course I'll do my best and double best. But suppose my best is not good enough?"

"Oh, it will be," declared Kabumpo, giving the Red Jinn a little pat on the back with his trunk. "I'll bet on your red magic any day in the year. Look at the way that elixir saved Randy from the magic staff. Where is Planetty's staff, by the way— sort of dangerous to leave it about!"

"It's locked up safely in my iron cabinet," said Jinnicky, closing one eye. "So you really think I'm good, old Gaboscis—better even than the Wizard of Oz, eh?"

"Oh, much," asserted the Elegant Elephant, wagging his head positively.

"All right, then, leave me—leave me," begged the Red Jinn, fairly pushing them out of the throne room. "I've ordered all my magic brought to me

here, and here I'll stay till this pretty little Princess and her charger come out of this metal trance. My, mercy me! Trance—entrance—entrancing. Oh, har, har, har! I've an idea there, my boys!" Bouncing off the sofa, Jinnicky skipped over to the Princess of Anuther Planet.

"Oh, Kabumpo! Do you think he really has?" whispered Randy, as he and the Elegant Elephant hurried through the door of the throne room and closed it softly behind them.

CHAPTER 19

Red Magic

THE hours Randy and Kabumpo spent waiting for Jinnicky to summon them to his throne room were the longest and most anxious they had ever endured.

"Even if he does restore them," groaned Randy, pacing feverishly up and down one of the garden paths, "he'll have to send them straight back to Anuther Planet." Rumpling up his hair, he looked wildly back at the Elegant Elephant, who was just behind him. "And if they go," declared the young

241

Chapter Nineteen

King in a desperate voice, "I warn you, Kabumpo, I shall jump on Thun's back and go with them."

"What? And leave ME?" gasped the Elegant Elephant, putting back his ears, "and your Kingdom and friends and all your responsibilities? No, no, Randy, this won't do. Besides, you'd probably perish in that outlandish metal wilderness with nothing to eat and no place to rest your head. You can't do it, my boy, and furthermore, I won't let you."

Snatching Randy up in his trunk, he held him as tightly as if he were already running away instead of threatening to do so. In the course of this bitter argument and as the young monarch began pummeling Kabumpo futilely with his fists, they were both lifted bodily into the air and set swiftly down in the Red Throne Room.

"The Master has good news for you," explained Ginger. "LOOK!" With his flashing white grin the little bell boy pointed to the throne itself and then, as was his wont, inexplicably vanished. What he saw made Randy rush forward and fling both arms round the Red Jinn's neck.

"Oh, you did it! You really did it!" he cried, embracing Jinnicky all over again. "How can I ever thank you enough?"

Chapter Nineteen

"Where am I?" murmured the clear silvery voice that Kabumpo and Randy knew so well. "Oh, what a netiful, netiful castle. Randy! Randy! And there you are, Big Bumpo, and Thun! But how did we come out of that debasement?"

Without bothering to answer, Randy seized Planetty's hands and looked and looked at her as if he were never going to stop.

"You're the same, and yet different," he mused, scarcely able to believe what he saw. "And Thun is the same, yet different, too."

"I am Thun the Thunder Colt, now, then, and always!" announced Thun, and gave a frightened jump, for he had actually spoken the words at the same time they went spiraling up into a sparkling sentence over his head. "Oh, Princess, Princess!" he whinnied joyously. "Do you hear? Do you see? I can talk, I can hear, I can see and hear myself talking!"

At each word Thun gave an ecstatic bound and then began racing madly round and round the throne room, in and out between the red pillars, leaping over chairs and tables in a positively hair-raising fashion.

"Oh, my! Oh, my mercy me!" faltered Jinnicky,

and scooping up the Nonagon Cat, he jumped up on a red tabouret. "Stop him, somebody! Stop him!"

"Whoa, there! Come back here, Thun, come back; we want to look at you!" Running after the Thunder Colt, Randy caught him by his plumy tail and hung on till he actually did stop.

"And he doesn't make a sound when he gallops—

not a sound," marveled Jinnicky, edging nervously over to his throne and taking a seat beside Planetty.

"A sound but soundless steed! Har, har, har! And do not mind his breath, Randy, it cannot burn you now; it's cold fire and will not singe a thing!"

"But how did you do it?" demanded Kabumpo, touching Planetty lightly with his trunk.

"Oh, partly by my red incense, partly by my red reanimating rays, and partly by an old incantation against entrancery," explained Jinnicky, as Randy brought Thun back and handed him over to Planetty. "Do you feel all right now, my dear, and as beautiful as you look?"

"Oh, yes! Oh, very yes!" answered Planetty,

smiling shyly round at the Red Jinn. "And you, I know it now, you must be the Wizard so wonderful of Ev?"

"Wonderful! Wonderful? Well, I should say hay hurray!" Randy threw his crown up in the air and caught it. "Wonderful enough to save himself and us too. Oh, SO many things have happened, Planetty, since you and Thun turned to cold metal in that awful cellar!"

"I must make a note," muttered Jinnicky, patting Thun rather cautiously on the neck. "I must make a note to clean and cheer up that cellar. My! mercy! me! I haven't been down there for years!"

"And if I never see it again, it will still be too soon," grunted Kabumpo, leaning up against a red pillar. "Look, Jinnicky," he muttered out of a corner of his mouth as Randy and Planetty moved over to one of the windows and Randy began to tell the little Princess all that had happened on Nonagon Isle and Thun began kicking up his heels and talking to himself just for the fun of the thing. "Look, will these two have to go straight back to their own planet?"

"That is what is worrying me," Jinnicky said, speaking behind one hand and patting his hound, also released from its enchantment, with the other. "I managed to reawake and reanimate them, but, as you've probably noticed, they are changed. Most certainly they are alive, but no longer of living metal, see? The girl's hair is no longer of fine spun metal strands, but it is real hair, still silvery in color as her skin retains its iridescent sheen, but I'm very much afraid, as things are, that the Princess and her colt are unfitted for life on that far and rigorous planet of theirs. Yes," Jinnicky nodded his head emphatically, "I'm very much afraid they'll have to content themselves down here and live, eat and behave generally as natives of Oz or Ev."

"WHAT?" trumpeted Kabumpo so fiercely Nina jumped out of Jinnicky's arms and hid under the

red throne. "Oh, say it again!" he begged, swallowing convulsively. "Great Grump, why this is the best news I've heard since you've come up out of the sea."

"You mean they won't care?" exclaimed the Red Jinn, rubbing his palms nervously together.

"Care!" spluttered Kabumpo, waving his trunk toward the small red sofa where Randy and Planetty sat in rapt and earnest conversation. "They care for nothing but each other, old fellow. Right there, my dear Wizard, sits the future Queen of Regalia, or I'm a blue-bearded Nannygoat!"

"Oh, my, mercy me! You don't say! Oh, har, har, har! How delightful! Why, this calls for a celebration, a feast and a fiesta." Beaming with interest and benevolence, Jinnicky banged on the side of his throne with both fists and his elbows. "Prepare a feast," he ordered breathlessly, as Alibabble, his Grand Advizier, entered in a calm and dignified manner, showing no ill effects from his long months of servitude in the ruby mines. "Prepare a feast, Old Tollywog, there's to be a wedding, with rings, bells, palms, presents and all the fruity fixings."

"A wedding?" Alibabble looked sternly at his master, whom he instantly suspected of being the groom, then as the Red Jinn, grinning wickedly, waved to the engrossed pair on the red sofa, he nodded briefly.

"In that event," he remarked, backing rapidly away as he spoke, "I earnestly advise your Majesty to have a hair cut."

"Oh, my mercy me! Did you hear that?" screamed the Jinn, as he turned to Kabumpo, his face very red and angry.

"I certainly did," roared the Elegant Elephant, giving Jinnicky a playful little push. "Hasn't changed a bit, has he? And neither have you. The last time I was in this castle he was advising the very same thing."

"That's all he ever thinks of," fumed Jinnicky, fingering his long locks lovingly. Then as his eye rested again on the happy little Princess and the prancing Thunder Colt, his expression grew milder. "Randy! RANDY!" he called, jerking his thumb imperiously at his royal guest. "See here, my boy," he explained, puffing out his cheeks importantly, as Randy came to stand beside the throne. "I have done MY part to save your little Princess and now you must do yours! Unfortunately," Jinnicky's face grew long and dolorous, "unfortunately, Planetty and Thun, from this time on, will be unable to exist on Anuther Planet, so now, without a home or country, what will become of them?" In mock distress the Red Jinn stared down at his young friend.

"Oh, Jinnicky! How wonderful! Oh, Jinnicky, do you mean it? Thank you! Thank you! THANK

YOU!" Pressing the little Jinn's hands, Randy went racing across the throne room.

"Planetty," he whispered breathlessly in the little Princess' ear. "How would you like to be Queen of

Regalia, to go back to Oz with Thun, Kabumpo and me and live in my castle for always?"

"Oh, I think—" Planetty's soft yellow eyes fairly danced with surprise and happiness—"I think that would be very nite. Oh, Randy, that would be netiful, netiful!"

CHAPTER 20

King and Queen of Regalia

THE feast to celebrate Randy's and Planetty's wedding was the grandest and merriest in all the merry annals of Oz and Ev. It was, in fact, a double celebration. The Red Jinn's return and his victory over Gludwig was enough to keep his subjects cheering for days and to honor his rescuers and especially the little Princess of Anuther Planet and her royal consort, the Evians outdid themselves, putting on one show after another. There were parades and pageants, fireworks and speeches and so many presents and parties it makes me jealous

253

just to think of them. Over and over again Planetty and Thun rejoiced in their new life and way of living, and eating the delicacies prepared by Jinnicky's chef was not the least of its privileges. In the Red Jinn's castle eating was a pleasure as well as a necessity. But after a month's merry stay, during which every point of interest in Jinnicky's

vast realm was visited, the travelers bade the little Jinn a hearty and affectionate adieu.

Mounting Kabumpo and Thun, and laden with gifts and good wishes, the young King and Queen set out for the Land of Oz and their own royal castle. Uncle Hoochafoo had already received his instructions and as Randy had predicted things were very gay, very different and very cozy in that regal and mountainous little Kingdom. Planetty's staff, powerful as ever, was a great help and protection to the young rulers and the small red hand bag that packed itself went on many journeys with the little Queen of the country.

If this story were beginning instead of ending, I could tell you a whole book of adventures they had traveling with Kabumpo and Thun through the great Land of Oz, for these days the Elegant Elephant spends almost as much time with Randy and Planetty as he does with the Royal Family of Pumperdink, and most of it in travel. And in Oz, what a gay way one travels! The other morning as I lay dreaming of them all, I got to thinking how nite it would be if the horses on milk wagons here were all soundless gallopers like Thun!

THE END